I0639635

BRUTAL BOSS

WILLOW FOX

CHAPTER ONE

MADISYN

STANDING OUTSIDE STEELE CONCIERGE MEDICAL, I stare up at the tall, white building as it towers above me. I feel small and insignificant in comparison, but my contribution is more than just as a nurse.

"Waiting for something?" Hannah asks.

I take a swig from the cup of coffee in my hand. "The caffeine to kick in?" I was waiting for my colleague with the FBI, Special Agent Savannah Blakely, to make contact. She never did show up at the coffee shop.

Hannah grabs my arm and drags me in through the front door, oblivious to the fact that I secretly work for the FBI as a forensic nurse.

We show our badges to security before being granted entrance past the lobby for the elevators.

"Check out the eye candy at six o'clock," Hannah whispers to me as we approach the long hallway of elevators. There are eight elevators, four on each side, making it so that no one has to wait too long for a ride up to their floor.

I suppose when you pay twenty-five thousand dollars a person per yearly enrollment fee, the least they can do is not make it a long wait to see your physician.

I inconspicuously glance in the direction Hannah suggests. A gentleman with a dark, scruffy beard, dark eyes, and tattoos covering his arms, chest, and up to his neck meets my stare.

It's Mikhail Barinov, my target.

Is that why Savannah bailed on my ass this morning? Did she see him enter the building on her way to the coffee shop?

I wouldn't expect a text or phone call from her. My FBI-issued cell phone is at my desk in the city. I have a burner phone that the bureau provided me with, and Savannah has direct orders not to use that phone number. Contact between us is kept to a minimum.

"Hot, right?" Hannah says with a wicked grin. "I hope he ends up as one of my patients today. I'd love to do a full physical exam on him."

"I never took you for the tattooed, bad boy type," I say. She's got a boyfriend at home. He's sweet, charming, and an accountant. There's not much of a fantasy wrapped up in that package.

Hannah is a ray of sunshine, and Mikhail is positively trouble. Thankfully, she's just looking and not going to ask for his phone number.

The elevator doors ding open. Hannah shuts her mouth, I do the same, and we step inside first.

Mikhail shuffles in as well, his suit coat off, draped over his arm. Accompanying him, is a bodyguard or one of his men. He has a half-dozen bodyguards based on the intel I reviewed before my undercover assignment.

I don't specifically recognize the gentleman, but Mikhail did a short stint in prison awaiting his trial. It's possible he made some new connections and grew his empire.

Neither appears to be injured or unwell at first glance. But Mikhail and his buddy could also be visiting a patient.

Or maybe he's making sure he didn't catch anything while behind bars. Who the hell knows why he's showing up today?

The man in the prestigious suit coat presses the button to the third floor. There are a wide array of physicians and medical offices on the third floor. It doesn't narrow down his reason for coming in today.

"Any lunch plans?" Hannah asks me, her mood downright chipper. Although she's talking to me, she's ogling the bratva leader. I'm confident that she has no idea who he is, or if she did, she'd shut it down right now.

"Just grabbing sandwiches with my new bestie?" I say, nudging her shoulder. "Assuming that we can get away for an hour."

Hannah chuckles. "You're lucky if you get a fifteen-minute break."

My first assignment is to connect with Mikhail without appearing like I genuinely want to. If he senses that I'm desperate, he'll see right through the charade. It must seem genuine, which is why he'll need to make the first move.

That's a tough sell in the elevator when he doesn't know anything about me.

But he's seen me.

That's the first step.

And now that he'll recognize me, hopefully, I can earn his trust.

The elevator dings, and Mikhail steps out along with his muscle, pretending that he didn't even notice us or acknowledge our existence.

Except he did notice me.

His gaze locks with mine downstairs, and while I have to pretend it's all business, there is something there. A spark that shouldn't have been, and a stirring of feelings that make my stomach flutter and my heart rate quicken.

After the double doors shut, I shoot a look at Hannah. I can't tell her he's bratva, but he gives off the bad boy vibe. "You and bad boys with tattoos?" I joke.

"My parents sent me to boarding school. I guess I'm still rebelling."

"Well, you'd better get it out of your system. Any day now, Mark is going to propose."

———

I've never been deep undercover. I did a week-long stint with the Sanchez Cartel eighteen months ago, but I didn't come anywhere close to their leader, and that's nothing compared to the viciousness of the bratva.

After work, I catch a glimpse of Agent Blakely outside. Savannah is keeping a low profile, but the moment I lock eyes with her, she gives me the signal for the second stage of our plan.

While I've been working diligently at the medical center as a nurse, the team back at the New York City field office has been digging up information on the bratva and gathering up intelligence to analyze.

I head down the block to grab my car, destined to break down on my way home. The vehicle will overheat, and the engine will die a few blocks from the bratva's compound if I'm lucky.

They had to pick the crappiest, coldest, and rainiest day in existence.

Some days, my job sucks.

I pull out of the parking garage and head down the block. Traffic is heavy, which isn't uncommon for New York. If I weren't undercover, I'd ordinarily take the subway to the FBI field office from my house.

But as Madisyn Taylor, I drive to work daily in a used car that the agency purchased. Surprisingly, the vehicle still has four wheels attached, but it's well over two hundred thousand miles, and the outer body is an eyesore with its rust and paint discoloration.

Are nurses at the concierge center not paid well? It looks like I'm living paycheck to paycheck.

Is that the impression they want Mikhail to have? That I'm destitute and for him to take pity on me.

I have memorized the directions to the bratva compound, and the rental property that I'm staying in is located a few miles past the location.

Rain pelts the windshield, and I pop on the wipers, struggling to see through the onset of weather. I'm not looking forward to what comes next.

I'm a bundle of anxious energy, which I have to contain if I want this to go without a hitch. I've trained for this moment, going undercover, being able to rattle off a lie without being caught.

Heading down the road and away from the city's dense traffic, my check engine light pops on. I hit the gas a little harder, hoping that I'll be able to make it to my destination before the deluge outside drowns me.

The engine sputters, and the oil light pops on next. The FBI really wanted to make sure my car broke down. The engine produces a horrible clicking sound and dies just as I pull up within walking distance of the compound's fence.

I'd have preferred to be a bit closer. There are other nearby houses, but they're not the intended target.

I step out of the vehicle into the storm. It takes seconds for me to become soaked. I'm dripping wet, shivering, and my clothes are clinging to my skin.

I hustle toward the guard gate.

"Excuse me," I say. My teeth are chattering, and I'm not sure they can even understand the words coming from my mouth.

The guard pushes the window in his booth aside, sliding it to answer me. He's out of the rain, dry as a bone. "This is private property," he says. His voice is gruff, and he's got a thick Russian accent.

"My car broke down," I say and point at the vehicle a few yards away. I'm not sure if he can see it or not from his position inside of the booth, but he doesn't look the least bit concerned about helping me.

"Try your cell phone."

"It's dead." I pull my phone from my pocket. It's an older cell phone that the agency provided me with, a previous model that doesn't appear to give the same resemblance as a burner phone. The last thing I want is to draw more suspicion toward me.

If the battery hadn't been entirely drained earlier, then the deluge indeed killed my phone. I show it to the guard on duty.

He grumbles and picks up the landline phone. "I'll call a tow truck for you," he grunts.

As I stand out in the cold, shivering, soaking wet, with the rain continuing to pour, a black SUV with tinted windows pulls up to the gate.

The driver's window rolls down, and I recognize the man from earlier at the hospital, the bodyguard. Mikhail Barinov is seated in the front passenger seat.

The bodyguard doesn't say a word. He doesn't have to. My presence is enough to warrant an explanation.

"The girl says her car broke down," the gentleman in the booth answers. He opens the gate for their vehicle.

Thunder bellows out overhead.

Mikhail steps out into the deluge with an umbrella and hurries around to the passenger side to open the door for me. He slips out of his black wool coat, which is mostly dry, and drapes it over my shoulders. It's a warm and welcome relief from the cold clothes that cling to my skin.

"Come inside, dry off, and we'll get you on your way," he says and opens the back door.

I am shivering and trembling from the frigid weather. The coat keeps me from making a mess of the leather interior with my wet clothes. "Thanks," I say, and Mikhail shuts the door before stepping around to the passenger side.

The engine purrs as the driver hits the gas and guides the SUV forward past the open gates.

Shivering, I shove my arms into the warm coat and my hands into the pockets to get warm. My fingers graze over a small metallic rectangular object, a flash drive.

CHAPTER TWO

MIKHAIL

IT'S RAINING OUTSIDE, pouring, and some girl who barely looks old enough to drink is standing by my gate.

Maybe she's older than twenty-one. It's honestly hard to tell with her blonde hair clinging to her body.

It still feels like winter, except it's not snowing.

Where the hell is her coat? Or at the very least, an umbrella?

There is an abandoned vehicle not twenty feet away, its hazard lights flashing. That car should be put out of its misery. It's probably older than the vanilla-blonde-haired girl in the back seat of the SUV.

Luka doesn't look the least bit pleased to be bringing her inside the compound, but it is on my orders, and I'm the fucking Pakhan around here. I make the shots and tell my men what to do.

Luka is a good bodyguard. He obeys my commands and is loyal to a fault. He'd have married my sister and been given my blessing if she wouldn't have turned on the family. That little brat runs with the Italians. She dared to have me arrested and put behind bars.

That's not to say she didn't have her reasons, but I'm no ordinary man. I run the bratva. I'm the Pakhan, the boss of the entire operation. My work is my life, and my family consists of my men. Their blood runs with mine.

I won't be imprisoned, and neither will they.

I rule New York City, and I don't intend to let anyone or anything stand in my way.

"Come inside, dry off, and we'll get you on your way," I say as I open the door for her and invite her into the back seat.

Her teeth are chattering and slightly blue.

"Thanks."

I loan her my coat, trying to keep the back seat from becoming a pool, and help warm the girl up.

Luka pulls around to the garage entrance to keep us from getting wet. After he pulls the vehicle inside, he opens the back door for her to step out.

"Come with me," I say, having her follow me into the compound.

Ordinarily, I wouldn't let a stranger inside my home. Ivan would be expected to handle anyone outside the gate, but I'm feeling generous, and I find her soaking wet to be fucking hot.

She's shivering and cold. The girl is vulnerable. I like women who are defenseless and weak. Not because I want to hurt them. No, I'm not that kind of monster.

I can help them and offer them a life they couldn't ordinarily have—an opportunity.

But this girl hasn't given any indication of her helplessness other than her broken-down vehicle, which did look pretty damn pathetic.

"I'm Mikhail," I say, introducing myself as I open the door and lead her inside. "You should take off your shoes."

She slips them off with ease. They're black and slip-on, practical, which I'm not used to seeing. Usually, the girls who visit me wear fuck-me pumps and sexy boots that lace halfway up their legs.

Her socks are soaked and squish under her feet.

"Socks off too. I can't have you making a mess in this place," I say.

She obliges without so much as a word. She leans against the wall, and I grab her arm to steady her. I don't need a giant wet butt print on the walls.

"Name," I say when she hasn't introduced herself yet. I'm a bit more forceful, but she's focused on the task of removing one sock at a time.

Her toes are ghastly white from the wet clothes, which look even more stark against her bright red painted toenails.

"I'm Madisyn," she says, her teeth chattering.

I steady her back onto her feet after her socks are removed.

"You're soaking wet and need to get out of your clothes," I say. I help her remove the coat I loaned her, and she doesn't object.

Will she object when I tell her that she will have to remove everything in front of me? I can't take a chance that she's a cop or some girl wearing a wire trying to get information and have my ass thrown back in jail.

I'm doing everything I can to turn my life around. Well, stay out of prison anyway. It's not like I'm going to start doing good deeds and being a good guy and all that shit.

That's not how I operate.

Luka follows inside behind us. He glances briefly at Madisyn before heading down the hallway without so much as a word.

He knows to keep his mouth shut, but he's not the least bit thrilled that I brought a stranger into my home.

Well, it is my home, and I can invite anyone I want inside. Besides, the girl is practically helpless and would get hypothermia before a tow truck shows up.

The sun is beginning to set, and the rain will undoubtedly turn to black ice. They're calling for an ice storm tonight.

The blonde girl exhales a soft breath after I remove her wet coat.

"Come with me," I say, ordering her to follow.

Wordlessly, she accompanies me down the hallway and stops as I begin the climb up the stairwell. "Where are you taking me?" she asks.

I stop on the third stair and turn around to face her. "You need to get out of those wet clothes."

Madisyn's hair is wet and tangled against her skin. Her clothes cling to her body, making her bra see-through and giving me an ample view of her breasts through the white cotton shirt.

She wraps her arms around herself, shivering.

"Come now, or I'll carry you," I say.

Her brow tightens, and she opens her mouth like she's going to make some smart-ass remark. But instead, she grunts her answer, "Fine."

Madisyn follows me up the stairs, and I escort her into my bedroom. Usually, I'd frisk a girl, make sure that she's not hiding a weapon or wearing a wire, but it's considerably apparent there isn't much under her clothes.

Even so, being a bratva boss, one can never be too careful.

"Strip," I command.

"What?" Her fingernails are digging into her forearms, her hands clenched.

"You need to get out of your wet clothes, and I need to make sure you're not harboring a weapon," I say. I forego the part about wanting to ensure she's not wired. There's no reason to scare her. She has no idea what I do for a living.

I stalk across the length of the room and open the drawer, retrieving a black t-shirt and sweatpants. They'll be too big on her, but there's a drawstring she can use to tighten them a bit.

In the meantime, I can have one of my men throw her clothes in the dryer while she warms up inside the house.

"Can I use the bathroom?" she asks, holding out one hand for the clothes I've acquired from the dresser.

"No. I wasn't joking about the weapon."

"I wasn't joking about changing in the bathroom," Madisyn says.

There's a fire behind her gaze, and I hate to admit I like it a lot. It's unheard of that anyone challenges me, and even rarer that it's a woman.

My gaze moves over her wet clothes again. "You were at the medical center today," I say, recognizing her from the elevator.

"I'm a nurse," Madisyn says.

"Then you know that this is strictly business and can appreciate detaching from a situation."

Her jaw drops, surprised by my remark. "You aren't serious? I'm not changing in front of you."

"Then I guess you're not getting the dry clothes."

She's shivering. There are goose pimples on her arms, and her lips are tinged blue.

The girl is probably trying to think warm thoughts, pretend that she's warm, but there are obvious signs of her distress, and eventually, she'll succumb to my demands.

"Fine," she says and turns for the door to the hallway.

Damn, she's stubborn!

I grunt and throw my head back. "Madisyn!" my voice echoes and booms.

A shiver runs through her, visible as she stands in the doorway, her back to me. I don't think that last shudder was from the cold, but the rest probably is. Her teeth are chattering.

"Strip, or I will undress you myself," I say and stalk across the wooden floor, slamming the bedroom shut. "Happy? Now you have privacy."

My guards don't need to see her naked, but I need to ensure that she isn't carrying something that she shouldn't.

Her bottom lip trembles. I assume it's the cold, and she's bluer than when she first stepped foot inside the compound. The place is plenty warm, but with her icy cold and wet clothes clinging to her body, she's not likely to warm up.

Her hands move to the hem of her shirt, but she's trembling. It will take all night at this rate, and I'm not a patient man.

I approach her, my hands warm against her icy skin. I let my fingers cover hers and guide her shirt and her hands up and over her head.

She covers her breasts the moment the shirt is in my hands and off her body.

"You're going to have to take that off, too. Anything you're wearing that's wet won't help you get warm," I say.

Madisyn presses her lips together and glances past me. She smells like a rain shower, like the outdoors.

I exhale a heavy breath. Her scent is intoxicating and makes my heart hammer in my chest. "Bra comes off. So do your skirt and panties."

"Can't you at least look away? You can see I'm not carrying a weapon," she says.

"I'm no gentleman," I warn her. There's no point in pretending to be something that I'm not.

The color comes back into her cheeks, but I can't tell if it's from embarrassment or anger. She appears defeated and reaches behind herself, unclasping her bra, holding the thin beige lace in her hands. Madisyn pushes her skirt down and then her panties, dropping her sopping clothes to the floor.

"Can I have something dry to wear now?" There's a terseness to her tone.

I smirk and head into my bathroom, retrieving a clean, dry towel for her to properly dry off before handing over the clothes that she can wear until her own dry.

Bending down, I pick up her wet linens. "Stay in here," I order and slip out into the hallway.

Nikita heads up the stairs. "Everything okay, boss?" he asks. By now, word that I brought a stray in has probably reached everyone's ears.

"Put these in the dryer. There's also a pair of socks by the garage entrance that need to go in."

"Of course, sir. Anything else?"

"I want you to run background on the girl, Madisyn."

"Any chance you have a last name?" My request doesn't amuse Nikita.

Well, tough shit. I don't want to make it obvious I'm checking up on her. Running into her twice in one day strikes me as a little more than a coincidence.

I want to be wrong.

"She's a nurse at Steele Concierge Medical. I'm sure you can look up the staff on their website: blonde hair, deep brown eyes. Luka got a look at her. Run any photographs you see by him."

"On it." Nikita grabs the garments and heads down the stairs. I wait a second before breezing right back into my bedroom.

Madisyn already has the black t-shirt on and is lifting the waistband of the sweats as I enter. She secures the drawstring, making the pants fit better than I imagined. They're still several sizes too big on her, but she looks dynamite in my clothes.

"One of my staff put your clothes in the dryer. Why don't we head downstairs and contact a tow company?"

"That would be great."

I open the bedroom door, and she follows me out and down the stairs. I lead her down to the study and leave the pocket door open.

There's a landline in the study and another in the kitchen. They're rarely ever used, and I have repeatedly considered dropping the line, but money isn't an obstacle.

"I don't suppose you have a phone book?" she asks with a laugh.

"I can't believe you're old enough to know what that is," I say, glancing her over. I pull my cell phone from my pocket. "I'll give you a number that you can dial. He's a friend."

"Thank you."

CHAPTER THREE

MADISYN

SLEIGHT OF HAND. Isn't that how magicians keep their tricks from being revealed? Apparently, I'm not too bad at it, either.

My cousin gave me a magic kit for my seventh birthday, and it turns out it's the best gift that I ever received.

The thumb drive moves from my hand to my palm, to the tips of my fingers. Thankfully, it's incredibly small, and Mikhail hasn't noticed that I have it in my possession as he searches every inch of me.

I need to do something with it and store it some place until I leave, which could take some time. I'm supposed to call Agent Lexington on a number that's being routed to appear as a tow company if anyone investigates the call.

Except Mikhail is giving me the number of someone he knows, and if his friend shows up, how will I explain the situation? I need to get close with Mikhail, not blow my cover at the first opportunity possible.

I dial the number Mikhail relays to me and wait for someone to answer. Except it rings endlessly. I shake my head. "It's just ringing." I've lost count of how many times the phone has rung, but they don't have voicemail to leave a message.

Relief floods through me. "Do you have another number? Someone else we can call?" I suggest, hoping that he takes the bait.

"I'll text him," Mikhail says, and gestures for me to hang up the phone.

My hair is still damp and sticking to my clean, dry t-shirt, making me chilly. There's a fireplace on the opposite wall, but it's not turned on.

I approach the fireplace. There are fake logs, and it looks like a gas fireplace.

"Does it work?" I ask, hoping it produces heat. I'm still cold from the rain. It doesn't help that my hair is damp. I rub my hands together, trying to warm myself up.

Mikhail strides across the space between us and reaches for the switch on the wall. Immediately, the fire comes to life.

There's a warmth that radiates from the fake flames. My nose tickles with the smell. It has a faint odor of gas, but it seems to dissipate after a few seconds. "Thank you," I say.

He grabs a throw blanket tucked away in a drawer and drapes it over my shoulders like a shawl. "You might want to borrow this for a bit, too," he says.

While his demeanor is gruff, the simple act of kindness feels almost unnatural. But I take the blanket, nevertheless. I'm freezing, and it offers me a bit of warmth to get comfortable.

"I have to admit..." Mikhail's voice is low and rumbly. He folds his arms across his chest. His gaze latches on me.

I wait for him to speak and pull the blanket tighter around myself. My hands clutch the scratchy navy fabric.

"I would have expected Steele to pay their nurses better."

I tremble from the chill in the air, along with his icy words. "What do you mean?"

How does he know what I make? Or what I supposedly make for a living.

"That piece of shit car outside," Mikhail says and gestures with his thumb toward the front of the building where I broke down.

"I don't have the best credit," I say, thinking up an excuse as quickly as I can. "And aside from the monthly payments, the interest is just obnoxious."

He lets out a slight huff, and his gaze narrows. "Well, then you'd better learn to pay your bills on time. You're not going to make it into work with that hunk of metal sitting in front of my house."

"I'll pay to have it towed," I say.

"You will pay, but not with money," Mikhail says.

I can't believe the nerve of him! Does he think I'll just fall into his bed because I'm under his roof?

"Excuse me?" I remove the blanket, no longer cold.

No, I'm steaming. Fuming with rage as I break the distance between us and come to stand toe-to-toe with him. My hands are balled into fists, and I shove the blanket at his chest.

"You heard me," Mikhail says, a snicker on his face. "You come into my home, wear my clothes, and use my phone. You can expect to owe me something in return."

"Owe you?" I'm appalled by his suggestion, and I downright ought to be. "I'll be going," I say and brush past him for the open door into the hallway.

Mikhail grabs me by the arm. "You're not going anywhere without my permission."

"Excuse me?" Who the hell does he think he is? I yank my arm and attempt to break free from his grasp, but his hold on me tightens. "Let me go," I seethe.

His darkened stare glides down my body. "And you'll go where, exactly? Your shoes are soaked. Your clothes are in my dryer. And if you've forgotten, it's still raining outside. The streets are icy by now, and no one is coming to get you," Mikhail says.

My shoulders slump at his words.

Defeated.

I feel like he's treating me as though I were a child, berating me for having a temper tantrum of some sort. Except this isn't an outburst. It's me trying to get away from the monster towering over me.

He blocks my escape, his body large enough to keep me from slipping past him and into the hallway.

"I'll walk home," I say, staring up into his cold gaze. "I'm not afraid of a little rain." Does he think I'll melt?

"It's icy and dangerous outside," Mikhail reminds me. "You're lucky your car broke down and you didn't crash into something outside. Now, come with me." He grabs my hand and pulls me out of the study.

I wanted to leave that room, but now that he's in control and dragging me through his enormous home, I don't want to follow him.

"Get off me!" I try to shrug out of his grasp, but his hands are massive, and he's strong. A few maneuvers I learned at the academy in Quantico could take his ass down, but I don't want him suspecting that I'm a federal agent.

Instead, that leaves me with being dragged by this mammoth of a man. Hairy. Beastly. And not the least bit pleasant to be around.

"You could say thank you, Mikhail," he quips, mocking me. "I did save your life," he snarls at me, and I shudder.

There's a smile that shines in his eyes, a glint of humor and joy behind his darkened gaze.

"Thank you," I mutter under my breath.

"There, now was that so hard?" He lets go of my hand because his phone is buzzing in his pocket, and I yank myself farther back and away from him.

Mikhail either doesn't seem to care that I stepped away from him, or he's too busy reading his text messages on his phone to notice me. I glance toward the door. I could bolt outside and go where, exactly?

Would he come after me? If he did and one of my colleagues happens to pick me up, then everything that's happened is for naught.

I just have to deal with Mikhail a little while longer. Getting him imprisoned behind bars will make everything I deal with worth it in the end.

He shoves his phone back into his pocket, satisfied with whatever message was sent. "Tow truck will be here in the morning. He's got a half-dozen calls already because of the ice on the roads. You're staying here tonight."

My mouth goes dry, and my hands tingle, but I think it's because I'm still quite chilly from the cold. Having moved away from the fireplace and no longer having the blanket around my shoulders is making me uncomfortable.

I should have asked for a sweatshirt or something with long sleeves to wear. The house is enormous and, because of it, chilly. My feet are bare against the floor, and I could have used a pair of socks or slippers, something to keep me warm.

"I'm sure I can call a cab or a rideshare and find my way home," I say. I don't need him telling me what I can and can't do. He's a stranger, and even if I'm supposed to hunker down with him, get to know him and win his trust, it's not going to be by following his orders.

I'm not one of his soldiers.

I'm not Russian or bratva.

He shakes his head, pinching the bridge of his nose. "You can't just say thank you when someone is trying to do something nice for you?" Mikhail asks. He pins me with his stare.

My breath catches in my throat, and he steps closer. The blanket that I shoved at him earlier was still in one of his hands. He lifts his arms and wraps the scratchy wool over my back and around my shoulders.

"You look like an icicle," he says.

"I could use a pair of socks."

He raises an eyebrow. He seems surprised by my remark.

"The girl who insists she should leave wants something from me," he says.

I don't know whom he's talking to. His men seemed to have scattered the moment we stepped into the hallway together.

Mikhail is less forceful as he grabs my arm through the blanket and escorts me back into the study. The warmth from the hearth is much more evident with it having been left on the last several minutes.

I stalk toward the fireplace.

"Stay here," he says. "I'll get you a pair of socks."

"And a sweatshirt?" I ask.

"I'll see what I can do," Mikhail says. He turns and shuffles into the hallway. One of his men, Luka, the one from earlier in the vehicle, grabs his attention.

They step aside, their voices low. I try to inconspicuously listen in to their conversation, but it's not easy several feet apart. If I step closer, I might catch a bit of the discussion, but Mikhail is bound to wonder why I'm not by the fire.

With one hand, I keep the blanket cinched shut and the thumb drive in my grasp, and with the other, I let the fire warm, trying to make me toasty.

I'm left alone. The two men bustle down the hallway, and I can't tell if Mikhail is going up the stairs to grab me a pair of socks or if he's accompanying Luka and something else is going on instead.

It's not as though Mikhail trusts me. I can't come out and ask him what's going on. We're strangers. I'm lucky that he's not throwing me outside into the storm.

I glance out the window. It's hard to see much of anything. A blanket of darkness surrounds the property.

"I brought you something," Mikhail says. He's carrying a blanket and pillow. "You can sleep in here, by the fire," he says.

He brings the items to the sofa and puts them down, shutting the curtains.

"I don't get a bedroom?" The place is enormous. He's bound to have an extra bedroom or two not being used for the night.

He huffs under his breath and barges in on my personal space, stealing the heat of the fire with it as he blocks my view of the amber glow.

"You get what I give you," he says roughly.

I glance at the sofa. There are worse places that I could be right now, including in the rain or trying to drive home with black ice coating the roads.

"The couch is acceptable."

"That's a good girl," he says with a wry grin. "I'll have one of my men retrieve a pair of socks and sweatshirt for you to wear. In the meantime, our private chef has prepared dinner. You're welcome to join me."

I'm not hungry. Being under the bratva's roof has raised my adrenaline levels and made me lose my appetite. "I think I'll just head to bed."

Mikhail's brow furrows, and he glances at his watch like he's really making sure he's not losing his mind. "Nonsense. You will join me for dinner. I'm not asking."

He's irritating. I'll give him that.

"What kind of host would I be if I didn't feed my guest?" Mikhail asks.

I pause. He's right. He doesn't know who I am, that I'm cautious around him because I know he's a monster who has murdered men and threatened children and their families.

Taking anything from him is dangerous, and the thought that he could poison me isn't the least bit reassuring. But what choice do I have? He will grow suspicious if I don't eat, and I hate to admit that I am hungry.

"Thank you." I force a smile past my lips, and he escorts me out of the study and down the hallway until we reach the dining room.

There's an elegant table, set with dinnerware for two. Was he expecting other company? "What about your men?" I ask. "Don't they eat with you?"

"They dine when I'm done," Mikhail says. "At least for tonight."

I purse my lips, and my gaze tightens. "This isn't a date," I say. I don't want him getting any filthy ideas about what might transpire between us.

"I wouldn't dream of it." He escorts me to my chair and pulls it back, waiting for me to sit.

I'm underdressed with sweats and a t-shirt on while Mikhail is in a deep black suit. He looks striking, albeit scary, but there's something about him that I find quite unusual in a pleasant way.

He pushes my chair in, and I catch my breath, startled by the gesture.

Mikhail leans in, and his breath tickles my ear as he stands behind me. "Relax, I'm not going to bite."

But he could. He's the kind of man who would rip a man's ear off if given a reason. Maybe he doesn't even need a reason. Men like Mikhail gain power through fear and violence.

My feet are firmly planted on the floor. I still don't have socks, and the floor is cool against my toes. I've gotten used to the chill, the light, feather-like hair standing up on my arms. "I wasn't thinking you were," I say.

I don't let him see fear. He probably derives his power from the terror that he exudes. My team knows I'm here. They won't let anything happen to me.

Except I'm not wired. There are no cameras or listening devices implanted inside the building. No one can see or hear me if I call for help.

I'm deep undercover, and there's no getting out.

"You seem distracted," Mikhail says.

"Just overwhelmed," I say. It isn't a lie.

"How so?" he asks and opens a bottle of red wine on the table. He pours himself a glass and then glances at me. "You are twenty-one, correct?"

I doubt he cares whether I'm old enough to drink or not, but I appreciate the compliment.

"Well over." His remark is enough to lighten the mood for a moment, and he pours me a glass.

"Thank you." I want to grab the glass and down the dark red liquid, but I wait for Mikhail to take the first taste.

Not that I suspect it's poisoned. I just don't want to seem rude.

He pulls out the wooden chair and takes a seat at the other place setting at the table. There's no food out yet. I presume his staff will be bringing it to us.

"What do you do for a living?" I ask.

I don't expect him to be forthright and confess all his sins to me, but any ordinary girl would be curious as to the magnitude of his house and his supposed fortune.

"You mean how can I afford all this?" he asks, gesturing to the house. He lifts his glass and swirls the wine around, smelling the fragrant aroma before tasting.

I always thought you did that before pouring two full glasses, but the man is remarkable. That's for sure.

He inhales the scent deeply before bringing the glass to his lips.

I reach for mine and take a taste. It's dry but has no bitter aftertaste. It's a surprisingly decent wine.

"I'm a very lucky man," Mikhail boasts. "But enough about me. I like to know everything about the guests in my home. Tell me all about yourself."

I exhale a nervous breath. I have a decent cover story; I just have to make it believable.

CHAPTER FOUR

MIKHAIL

IT'S MORNING, and I groan, unpleased by the early hour. The sun hasn't risen yet, or if it has, it's buried under the thicket of clouds outside.

Is it still bitter and the roads icy?

I stalk out of bed, shower, and dress for the day.

Yesterday was interesting, with Madisyn. She's a girl whom I can't get out of my head, but I should. I don't need a sexy little distraction getting in the way of my work.

Besides, I'm not a man to form attachments to anyone, let alone engage in relationships.

Sex is something that I can handle and do rather well, but I don't need intimacy or the strings attached to it. And kids, lord help me if I have to ever see another one under my roof.

Before I was imprisoned, my sister had lived under my roof with her two children, fraternal twins, Sophia and Liam. Little obnoxious brats, getting into whatever trouble they could find. She and her twins ran off with the Italians, probably married the guy by now.

I'm not close with her.

How could I expect to be with her betrayal bleeding me from the inside out? She testified against me and tried to get me locked behind bars.

Well, she did technically get me locked up until I was released when it came back as a hung jury.

Yeah, I fucking did that, making sure my ass wasn't going to sit behind bars in a tiny cell for the rest of my life. Money and power have a way of getting me what I want.

I yank the curtains open, catching a glimpse outside. The sun is up, but it's buried behind the smoky gray clouds.

There's ice coating the trees, and the branches are heavy. We still have electricity, which is always a concern with winter storms when the power could go out. The compound is updated, modernized, but not new.

This place was first built in the late eighteen hundreds. It was expanded, remodeled, and kept up. But the power lines still come in from outside. They're not buried underground in this neighborhood.

We have a generator around the back if we need it, which helps our surveillance systems, handles the refrigerator, additional freezer, and other systems in the compound. It, however, is not a flawless structure.

There's a brief knock at the door. "Yes?" I call out, waiting for a response.

Nikita opens the door and steps into my bedroom. "Sir, you requested information on the girl, Madisyn Taylor."

"See, you were able to find her last name." I grin, pleased with Nikita's determination to gather my information as requested. "What have you found out?"

"Not much. She's a new hire, but her background checks out. She worked at a hospital for the past seven years in Ohio. I called the facility to make sure her work history is legit."

"Anything else?" I don't need to know the nitty-gritty details until there's something amiss. She mentioned over dinner that she recently moved to the city, but I hadn't pulled out of her where she was from.

"She's a nurse, but you already knew that. I don't think it's such a bad idea to keep her around," Nikita says, offering his opinion. "We could use a local on-call nurse when things get difficult."

The idea has certainly crossed my mind, but she's not a doctor, and her level of skill set, usefulness, and loyalty hasn't been proven to me.

"We have the concierge for that," I say, reminding him of our hefty investment in the organization. We don't just pay a monthly fee. We're also shareholders to ensure our privacy and who gets accepted as clientele. We don't want the Italian Mafia or the

Colombian Cartel showing up on the doorstep. They can seek out help elsewhere, like the local hospital or clinic.

"Dr. Gracie Steele?" Nikita asks, raising an eyebrow. "That woman is a straight arrow. If she gets any inkling of trouble, she'll go straight to the cops."

"She won't."

While Dr. Steele is a renowned surgeon and medical doctor, she's busy with her concierge medical practice, seeing patients, handling administrative functions, and downright swamped with day-to-day tasks. The woman wouldn't notice if we shared an elevator and one of our men had a gunshot wound.

She's preoccupied but not dumb. I'll give Nikita that much, but Dr. Steele isn't a physician we can use for a house call.

I trust her secrecy and privacy at the concierge facility, not inside my home.

"Fine, we'll get Madisyn's number and keep our options open, but only if it's an emergency. I don't like bringing in strays and feeding them," I say.

"Isn't that what you did last night?"

"Shut your mouth," I snarl at Nikita. He ought to watch his tone if he doesn't want to be reprimanded and given the toilets to clean or some other grunt work tasks that an errand boy could handle. "You're dismissed." I'm done dealing with him and want him out of my room.

"There is one other matter. Ms. Madisyn needs a ride to work this morning."

I exhale a heavy breath and reach for my phone on the bedside table. There are two missed text messages from Andrei, the associate who owns the chop shop downtown. He's the gentleman I attempted to get Madisyn to call last night, but he was busy with other vehicles that took priority.

"I'll handle it. Tell her I'll be down in five," I say, dismissing Nikita.

He wordlessly leaves the room, shutting the door on his way out.

I dial Andrei, waiting for him to answer the call. "Mikhail," Andrei says, recognizing my number. "Did you sleep in? Have a late-night?" he jokes, implying that I slept with Madisyn.

I grumble at his suggestion. "It's none of your business," I say with a hasty growl. One hand tightens its grip on the cell phone, the other balls into a fist at my side. "Did you tow her car?" I seethe between gritted teeth.

Andrei and I typically get along. I wouldn't have reached out to him if we didn't, but I don't need him making assumptions because he's a dick.

"I drove by this morning, but someone else picked it up already," Andrei says.

"Another towing company?" She had parked it on the side of the road. However, there was a no-parking sign nearby.

"Likely. Anyway, if you want to give me the plate number, I can call around and find out who towed it."

I throw my dirty clothes in the hamper and head out of the bedroom, shutting the door behind myself. "I'll text you the plate number as soon as I get it. Thanks, Andrei." I end the call and head down the stairs toward the study.

Madisyn sits up on the sofa, the blanket bunched around her waist.

"Did you sleep all right?" I ask.

"Yeah, the fireplace kept the room nice and toasty," she says. She's holding a steaming hot mug; I assume its coffee. One of my guards must have brought it for her. Her clean clothes are also at the bottom of the sofa, folded and ready to change into.

"What time do you have to work?" I ask. "I can give you a lift in this morning."

"That isn't necessary," she says, her cheeks reddening.

I take a step closer. Why is she blushing? What does she have to hide?

"How else do you plan on getting to work this morning? Unless you have the day off?"

She brings the mug to her lips and takes a sip. "No, I should go in for my shift. I was just hoping the weather was bad enough that I could have the day off."

"Does that ever happen?" I can't imagine a nurse gets any time off for weather. Maybe longer shifts when staff has trouble getting into work, but there aren't snow days or icy road days where the office is closed or opens late.

She smiles into her mug. "Never. Do you mind if I use the bathroom to change?"

"I'd rather you undress in front of me," I say.

Her eyes crinkle, and she smiles, shaking her head. "One show is your limit. Remember that," she says and stands.

She takes a swig, finishing the last drop of her coffee before pushing her empty mug at my stomach, forcing it into my hands.

There's an air about her today, a take no shit kind of attitude that she didn't show me yesterday. It's amusing to watch, to see her trying to take control when she has none while under my roof.

I'm in charge in the compound, and everyone damn well knows it.

My men all know it, and everyone who has ever associated with me as bratva understands I'm the boss.

But she's oblivious to the dark underworld nestled right under her nose. It's tempting, honestly, to show her a glimpse, a little peek, and see how she reacts.

Like giving her a taste of the forbidden fruit.

Madisyn reaches on the sofa to grab her clothes from the previous day. They'd been shoved into the drier after the deluge, but they're not the least bit clean.

"I'm going to see myself to the bathroom," she says. This time I notice that she's not asking permission. Since clearly, I wasn't giving her any bit of it.

She's sassy and quite a bit reckless. But she doesn't know what she's up against, who she's up against.

Which I find both irresistible and hot.

Madisyn brushes past me and heads out of the study and into the hallway. It takes her a second to get her bearings and remember her way around the compound. That's one of the advantages of having such an enormous home. It's easy for a new person to get lost.

And I don't want that to happen because she's bound to stumble onto something she shouldn't see.

I have men handling special projects for me, doing interrogations, laundering money, counting stolen goods, making counterfeit documents. It all happens under this roof. Maybe not simultaneously, but there are plenty of illegal drugs and weapons behind the pristine iron fence inside my compound.

I wait outside the bathroom door for Madisyn to finish getting ready. She's not like the other girls I've slept with, taking time to put on their makeup, do their hair, accessorizing, whatever the hell that means.

She's in and out of the bathroom in less time than it takes me to shave, and I have quite the beard-growing. I wait for her, and she seems jarred when she opens the door, seeing me on the opposite end.

"Sorry, did you need to use the bathroom?" she asks.

"No."

There's a sweetness and innocence to her. She's oblivious to the darkness and danger swooping down at her, circling and closing in to attack.

"Let's go," I say and lead her away from the bathroom, down the hallway, and to the garage entrance.

This time she has her socks on, and as we approach the door, she bends down to grab her shoes and slip them on.

"Are they dry?"

"Mostly, but they couldn't have gone into the dryer." She slips them on. I don my jacket and hat, along with a pair of gloves. The air outside is nippy, and in New York, you can never park close enough, even when it's valet.

"Come on, let's go," I say and escort her to the car.

"Sir," Luka says, hurrying to accompany us. He's typically my bodyguard these days and my driver when I'm away from the compound.

"It isn't necessary," I say and gesture for him to turn around. There are enough business errands to run and tasks to handle to keep Luka and my men busy while I'm away.

"Wow, no chauffeur?" Madisyn quips.

She's either careful not to refer to him as a bodyguard or doesn't realize that I need one. "Not today. Come on," I say, and open the passenger door for her as we approach the SUV.

I wait until she's in the vehicle before shutting the door. She's already buckled in by the time I climb into the driver's side. "I spoke with Andrei this morning," I say.

Hitting the garage button, I open the double doors and push the start button on the engine. It roars to life.

All the while, Madisyn gives me a peculiar stare. "Who?"

"My friend from the tow shop I contacted for you. He said your car was already gone this morning. If you give me the plate number, he can call around and find out who has your vehicle."

She opens her mouth and laughs softly. "I don't know my license plate number. Am I supposed to?"

"Well, that makes it a little more complicated," I mutter. My guy tries to do a good deed, and Madisyn is as clueless as can be.

"It has new plates. I just registered the vehicle since I moved here recently. Although it's not like I ever memorized my license plate in Ohio, either."

The girl gives off a country vibe. Like she's waited her entire life to live in the big city.

"Don't worry about it. I'll make a few phone calls," I say.

"That isn't necessary. I can deal with it during my lunch break."

I hit the gas, and we roll right out of the garage around the long, paved driveway toward the gated entrance. My men see the vehicle approach and have already opened the gate for us.

"When?" I overheard her conversation yesterday with her friend in the elevator. "Didn't you say you barely get a break, let alone a lunch hour?"

"You were listening!" Madisyn says with a laugh and pointing at me.

"Was I not supposed to be? We were stuck in an elevator together."

"I wouldn't use the word stuck," she quips. Her shoulders relax as she glances out the side window for a moment, and then her attention is dedicated back toward me. "Stuck implies that you couldn't be anywhere else, like the elevator was broken. But you were with me for what? Thirty seconds? Maybe a minute, including the time for the elevator doors to open and close."

"Well, I couldn't escape. So, stuck it is." I'm sticking to my guns. Why the hell not?

I'm never wrong.

No one ever questions the authority of a Pakhan. They know better, but this girl doesn't know anything about who I am and what I do for a living.

"Escape?" She stares at me and bursts out laughing. "You are crazy. Oh my gosh. I stayed overnight at a crazy person's house."

I glance at her briefly. "You're just figuring that out?" I ask, returning my attention to the road.

Traffic is getting heavy, and I don't need to slam into another vehicle because I'm paying more attention to the hot blonde sitting next to me.

"Usually, the response for that is thank you," I grunt.

Her brow furrows as she examines me, her eyes raking over my body. "You don't strike me as the kind of guy who looks for a lot of acknowledgments."

She isn't wrong. I don't need someone sucking up to me or patting me on the back for a job well done. "What makes you say that?" I shoot a look at her before gripping the steering wheel harder.

The SUV dings, and I bring my attention to the light on the vehicle's dashboard.

"Is there a problem?" she asks.

I need to fill up the SUV. Luka left us with barely any gas yesterday, and the fuel tank is nearing empty.

While the ice has melted from the road with the sun out, it's still frigid and the kind of job I'd have pawned off on Luka or any number of my men to handle.

"No," I grunt.

She leans closer and glances at the dashboard, noticing the fuel light. "It means you're almost out of gas."

"I know that." I glare at her. Does she think I've never driven a car before?

"You need fuel to make the engine go," Madisyn says, her face dead serious. "You can't drive a car without it. Like oil or wiper fluid."

"Oh my gosh. You're too much." I can't take it anymore, and she actually gets a chuckle from me. Was that her plan all along? To see me laugh. "Wiper fluid isn't a necessity."

"Well, it ought to be. When you're living in Ohio and after a snowstorm driving on the highway, you can easily run out of windshield washer fluid. Then it's dangerous if you can't see through the glass, especially when the sun is setting, heading westbound."

"Aren't you chatty this morning?"

"I did have two cups of coffee," she says with a reddening grin, like she's confessing to being naughty and in trouble. "I'm not normally allowed caffeine."

"Is that so?" I pull into the driveway of a gas station. "Sorry, it's going to get cold in here for a few minutes." I shut off the engine and step out into the brisk winter air to fill up the vehicle.

Every so often, I glance into the vehicle toward Madisyn. The tinted windows make it difficult to see much of anything.

I should drop her off at work and vow never to see her again. It's not like I'm doing her any favors by befriending her, and besides, I don't need any friends.

I'm a loner. I have my men to depend on, and that's more than enough. That's all I need.

Finishing up with filling the tank, I rush back into the SUV and out of the cold. "I've never been so grateful for Luka," I mutter.

"What's that?" Madisyn asks, giving me her undivided attention.

"Luka usually fills the tank up for me." I pull out of the lot and back onto the road. "What time do you get off work?"

"Are you asking me out?" There's a wry smile on her face.

Damn.

Does she hope that I'm asking her, because I wasn't?

"I was finding out what time you get off work so that I might drive you home."

She forces a smile. "I don't want to put you out more than I already have. I can have one of the girls give me a lift home."

"What time do you get off work?" I repeat the question. It's not that I need to run her around town or have my men accompany her. It's that Nikita is right. She is a nurse and having someone in our inner circle when we need it isn't such a bad thing.

Besides, I want the opportunity to get to know the woman I let crash on my couch. I won't be satisfied until I've seen the inside of her home, combed through her belongings, and am confident that she is one hundred percent authentic.

Generally, I have a decent indicator of bullshit and trouble. Madisyn falls high on the trouble meter, but I can't distinguish the difference between her causing me trouble because she's a woman, and I don't need a relationship, and her being trouble.

I pull up out front by the lobby near the entrance. "Eight-hour shift, you do the math," Madisyn says. She's upbeat, sunny, a little too normal for my taste.

"I'll be here."

————

Much of my day is spent discussing how to handle the cartel. They've been interfering in our dealings, trying to steal our business associates. Their men are dirty snakes, conniving con artists, and thugs.

We deal with plenty of shady individuals in our work. Still, the cartel prey on the elderly, scamming them into paying hundreds of thousands of dollars, wiping out their retirement accounts.

It's disgusting, and while I shouldn't care, I take pride in my work ethic, in what I do for a living. We may sell drugs and make a hefty profit, but we're giving them to folks who would otherwise get them from somewhere else. At least our drugs are high quality, none of that mixed shit with fentanyl.

My suppliers are like gold, and the thought of the cartel moving in to snatch our drugs or our suppliers doesn't bode well with me.

They've been talking with our suppliers, and that's enough to warrant action against them, strike while they're least expecting it.

If it's not the Italian mafia causing me a headache, it's the cartel. Not that we can't handle the problem. That's why I called a meeting with my men, to have them hit the cartel where it hurts.

They have orders to take out Carlos Sanchez, the cartel leader. Dmitri, my underboss, is running the operation. I've given him the go-ahead to put a hit on Sanchez.

Sanchez is not an easy man to get along with, but my men will do whatever is necessary to remove the problem.

I swing by Steele Concierge Medical after the meeting is finished. I make sure it ends, giving me enough time to get back across town to pick Madisyn up.

I should be ordering Luka or even Nikita to pick Madisyn up. But instead, I am behind the wheel.

Glancing at the clock in the vehicle, my fingers tap against the steering wheel. How long am I supposed to wait for her?

I glance in the rearview mirror. I'm always cautious about making sure that I'm not being followed.

That's why I typically have Luka drive. He's good with keeping an eye on being tailed while also focusing on the road.

I recognize one of the cartel's men hurrying inside the front entrance. He's not bringing anyone with him, and he doesn't appear as though he needs immediate medical attention, although he's certainly hightailing it like he might.

Is the cartel seeking the concierge's services? I'll need to have a word with Dr. Gracie Steele, and there are some clients I refuse to accept. The cartel is on that list.

I reach for my phone and text Nikita to investigate it for me. I want to know why the cartel is on our turf, using our facilities.

The double doors automatically open, and Madisyn breezes through like she's in a hurry. I shove my phone into my pocket, not wanting her to ask any questions.

Several people step outside behind her. One is a woman carrying a toddler, and another is a man by himself. He seems to have Madisyn in his line of sight.

Who is he?

He doesn't look like an employee, but maybe he's changed and done for the day. Could he be an ex-lover? Husband? No, if she were married, Nikita would have told me.

Madisyn heads toward my SUV and glances in the window before opening the door.

Smart girl, making sure it's me.

Then again, if she was smart, would she be taking a ride with a bratva boss?

She climbs into the front seat and slams the door, buckling her seatbelt. "Thanks for picking me up," Madisyn says. "I hope you didn't have to go out of your way."

"It wasn't a problem," I say, not answering her remark directly. "What's your address?" I ask.

She gives me her address, and I punch it into the GPS display, giving me directions. The route is straightforward and what I'd expect if I were going home. It has me drive right past my house.

"I managed to locate my vehicle," Madisyn says, killing the silence between us as I pull out onto the road.

"And word on what needs to be done to repair the car?" I ask, glancing briefly at her. I had meant to contact Andrei, but I'd gotten sidetracked this afternoon discussing Sanchez and the cartel.

"I need a new engine." Madisyn grimaces and folds her arms across her chest.

"It'll be cheaper for you to buy a new car," I say.

Somehow, I doubt that she can afford a brand-new vehicle, or she'd have already had one. A person doesn't drive a rundown piece of shit car for fun.

There's silent desperation that she exudes. She tries to hide the fact that she doesn't have money, that she's likely piss poor, but I'm not sure why. She has a decent job. Does she have debts that are burying her?

"Maybe a used car," she says, her voice soft.

I can't get Nikita's words from my head, suggesting that she could work for us and be available on call should the need arise. It would solve her money woes, but this isn't about her. It's about my needs, my men, our safety.

I need to know that I can trust her, and the only way to do that is to test her.

CHAPTER FIVE

MADISYN

ONE HOUR EARLIER...

"What are you doing here?" I ask, grabbing Aaron by the arm and pulling him down the hallway into an empty room.

I slam the door shut behind us.

Aaron Moore is my boss. He's not just my boss with the FBI, he's also every bit of a jerk, but I didn't know that when I slept with him. It was months ago, and in truth, it led me to take this assignment so that I wouldn't have to see him every day.

I requested a transfer out of his division, but I didn't exactly come clean with why I wanted a change. We both would have gotten into trouble, and while he instigated the entire affair between us, I wasn't innocent, either.

"Checking up on you," Aaron says. His hand reaches up, brushing a strand of hair behind my ear.

I push him away, trying to accomplish better boundaries between us.

"You can't just show up while I'm working." My teeth are clenched, and my jaw is tight. "You need to leave, and you can't come back here."

Does he not realize that he could break my cover? He could endanger my life by showing up and getting me made as an FBI agent.

The nerve of him not thinking about anything but himself! Typical Aaron.

"I need to leave? I'm taking you home, Madisyn. You don't belong here," he says and takes a step closer, invading my personal space. "Come back to work for the FBI. Come back with me."

Shit.

Does he not know about the undercover operation? Was he kept out of the loop and in the dark?

I open my mouth but shut it. If he doesn't know, then he's already on the outside, and I'm not about to ruin my career or my chance at making a supervisory agent someday.

"I can't do that, Moore. This is my new job, my new life." If he doesn't know that I'm undercover, I can't tell him. While I don't think he has any involvement with the Russian Bratva, my orders are to keep a low profile, and I can't do that with the FBI showing up at my new job. "You need to leave."

"There's a new team under my leadership, but I want you on it. They're a bunch of new agent trainees. I need someone I can trust on my team, someone who will have my back. Whatever happened between you and Kingston, I can go over his head. I can get you cleared and back on duty."

Supervisory Special Agent Barrett Kingston gave me the undercover assignment and he prepped me for the operation. Two of my colleagues who had worked under Moore are part of the assignment and, by the sound of it, are no longer on Moore's team.

I've barely been gone, and there have been a significant number of changes. What happened? Who did Aaron piss off to end up with trainees and having his entire devoted team reassigned elsewhere?

Is it a political move? Did Aaron piss off Barrett or another boss higher up? I doubt they got wind of the affair between us, or he'd have been out of a job completely.

It had been a mistake, sleeping with my boss. I'd been drawn to his power, to the influence over me, and been naïve to think that he might have loved me.

"You need to go. Our clients pay a premium for privacy, and they won't appreciate the FBI hanging around," I say, trying to reiterate without spelling it out that he needs to leave and never come back.

"Fine, but this isn't over, Madisyn." Aaron heads for the door. Grabbing the handle, he yanks it open. He doesn't so much as glance back at me as he stalks toward the elevator, shoulders slumped like he's been defeated.

If he knew why I was here, would he still fight for me to come back to the FBI? Or would he be supportive of my decision to work undercover?

It doesn't matter, he's a ghost of my past, and I need to let him go.

———

I get dressed out of my scrubs and back into my outfit from this morning. It's technically my clothes from yesterday, but the only person who seemed to notice was Hannah, and she thinks it's because I got laid.

Well, I didn't. But I won't elaborate on what happened, except my car broke down.

Which just has her even more suspicious.

"Are you going to tell me about your wild night?" Hannah asks as we head down the elevator together to leave.

"It wasn't wild. Just interesting, and no. Not right now," I say. The girl has no sense of boundaries.

"Pretty please?" Hannah begs. "My wild nights are chasing my toddler around and cleaning up after Mark. I swear it's like we're married, and we skipped the wedding and honeymoon. And don't even get me started on the diaper changes! Do not date a man who has a fear of changing a diaper."

"Yes, another reason not to have children," I say. "I clean enough bedpans around here. I don't want to do that at home."

Hannah rolls her eyes at me. "Oh, come on, it's not all bad. And that's not quite the same thing."

"I don't want to push the kid out of me!"

She chuckles at my fear. "You could always adopt?"

"Yes, I hear that puppies give wonderful kisses, and you can pay someone to clean up after your dog."

"You could hire a nanny to clean up after the baby?" Hannah laughs at her remark. "Why are we comparing babies to puppies?"

"You started it, talking about diaper changes." I scrunch my nose in disgust. "I'm with Mark on that one. Although on second thought, if I push a baby out of me, my husband damn well ought to change every diaper!"

"Good luck with that," Hannah says. "First, let's work on finding you a sexy boyfriend." She wraps an arm around my shoulder. "And when you meet him, I want every dirty detail."

I step out of the elevator, and the smile fades from my face.

Aaron Moore stands near the front entrance, his arms folded across his chest. The moment he lays eyes on me, he stalks toward me. I want to run, get away, but I'm not going to be that lucky. And Hannah will have a hundred new questions when she sees him.

"Madisyn, can I talk to you?" Aaron asks.

Hannah's eyes light up, and she releases his hold around me. "Oh, is this your mystery man from last night?"

I elbow her in the ribcage. "Okay, got it. I'll leave you two alone. I'll see you tomorrow," she says and waves, giving me a thumbs-up as she passes Aaron.

"I have somewhere to be," I say.

Hannah is already twenty steps ahead of me, and I can't use her as an excuse to ditch Aaron. I stop walking and come toe-to-toe with him. "Listen, it's over. It's been over. There's nothing between us anymore."

"I don't care about us. I mean, I do, Maddy, but we make a great team."

I swear if he says another word, I'm going to slug him. "You need to leave." I hurry past him, wanting to slip away.

I'm relieved when I spot Mikhail's vehicle parked by the entrance. I hurry away from Aaron, and I glance into the dark windows to make sure that I'm not opening the wrong vehicle's door and going with a stranger.

Although Mikhail technically is a stranger, he's also my mark. And this is my job, making him trust me.

Besides, I'd rather get into Mikhail's vehicle than Aaron's right now. Not that I think Aaron would hurt me physically, but he's stupid enough to get me killed.

Hopefully, Mikhail didn't notice Aaron, but at least he wasn't in his FBI attire—no suave suit to go with his audacious personality.

Mikhail and I make small talk about my shitty car and how I need a new vehicle. Yeah, with what money? Maybe he'll offer me a position and let me get closer to him. Not that I'm looking to sleep with the man. I've made that mistake once before with Moore.

I may not have been undercover with Moore, but both men exude power in a way that I felt highly arousing.

I have to tread carefully.

When Mikhail pulls up at my house, I smile sheepishly. The rental property is barely the size of his bedroom.

"Thanks for the ride," I say and pull my bottom lip between my teeth. I'm playing it coy, trying the shy approach. If I seem forceful, overbearing, or aggressive, I could easily push him away.

"It was my pleasure, but do you mind if I come inside? I need to use the bathroom," he says.

It's an excuse. We're not ten minutes from his house, and I doubt he has to pee that bad, but I take the bait.

I need the chance to connect further with him without it seeming like it's my idea. "Sure," I say.

He turns off the vehicle in my gravel driveway.

We step out, and I pull my keys from my purse, heading up the wooden porch stairs. They're creaky and old. They could use a new paint job. The porch is blue gray, along with the stairs.

I unlock the front door and hold it open for Mikhail. "Careful with the storm door—" I say, but before I can finish my thought, he lets it go as he enters, and it slams shut.

He glances over his shoulder at the door and mutters something under his breath.

"What's that?" I ask, stepping farther inside and slipping out of my shoes and coat. I flip the lights on inside the house and close the curtains since it's dark outside. No sense in letting the neighbors see inside my house.

There are two hidden cameras in case anything happens while Mikhail is in my home, but I don't suspect he'll do anything stupid. One camera is in the living room, the other in the bedroom.

So much for privacy.

"You need to have your stairs repaired and door fixed," he says. He glances around the house, taking all of it in.

"I left a message with the landlord, but I'm still waiting to hear back." I close the wooden door behind him and secure the lock.

"Typical."

"The bathroom is this way," I say, leading him down the hallway. I open the bathroom door and flip on the light.

"Thank you," he says.

He steps inside and shuts the door. I hear the latch click and saunter off into the kitchen to figure out what to make for dinner.

Should I invite him to stay over—for dinner? He's gone out of his way to give me a ride, let me stay at his place. It's strange to think that he's this big bad guy the FBI has made him out to be.

Could they be wrong?

Doubtful.

He probably is terrifying and a murderer, but he hasn't let me see that side of him. I open the pantry and shove the flash drive that I stole inside a box of cereal and out of sight. I'm still shocked and pleased that I was able to get it out of his house without him noticing.

I grab a pot and pan from the bottom cabinet. I've learned where everything is located so that it doesn't seem suspicious. The last thing I want is for it to look like I'm unfamiliar with my own house.

I put on a pot of water to boil noodles and grab several ingredients from the fridge to make a sauce for pasta.

The bathroom door clicks, and there are heavy footsteps against the floor. He's not the least bit silent on his approach.

I add some olive oil to the saucepan, waiting for it to heat up as I add some fresh garlic. "Do you want to stay for dinner?" I ask, glancing at him over my shoulder. I reach for the wooden spoon, mixing up the garlic to not burn on the stove.

His eyes are narrow and tight, fixated on me. I can't tell if it's a good or bad thing. "Who doesn't have any prescriptions in their medicine cabinet?"

I spin around to face him. He's just inches from me, towering above, demanding answers.

I point the wooden spoon in my hand at him. "Why are you snooping?" I accuse, turning the tables on him. Most people who snoop through a medicine cabinet don't start asking questions when they step out of the bathroom.

He grabs the spoon from me as if I were using it as a weapon and puts it down on the countertop, out of my immediate reach.

"I like to know who I associate with," Mikhail says. He's pinning me with his stare.

I lean up onto my tiptoes and grab him by his tie, pulling him down, crashing my lips against his, silencing him. If we're kissing, he can't ask any more questions.

"What are you doing?" he growls, pulling back, ending the kiss.

My lips tingle as I stare up into his darkened gaze. "You want to know who you associate with? Then get to know every inch of me," I say, challenging him to continue, to momentarily forget his question and focus on me.

I pull back slightly, still within his reach, as I yank my shirt up over my head and let it hit the floor.

I swear I hear another growl, this one much more guttural from the back of his throat. His eyes are black, his irises nearly impossible to distinguish from his pupils.

He stalks closer, his cold hands caress my bare skin, and I shudder in response. I don't have to fake being attracted to him. There's passion and power, a pleasure that sizzles through me.

The only room where there isn't a camera is the kitchen. I turn off both burners on the stove, not wanting to set the house ablaze.

His lips are on mine and fall to my neck, sucking and nibbling, tasting my skin. I push my pants down past my hips, letting them fall to the floor, toeing them off and away.

It's not like he hasn't seen me naked before, but this is different. This feels different. The last time I wasn't in charge, I didn't have a say in stripping down for him.

He loosens his tie and throws it on the floor with my clothes. His suit coat glides off, and he's undoing the buttons on his dress shirt when I tug the bottom of his shirt from his pants, my hands moving up his chest, touching his skin.

He's warm, and his muscles flex beneath my touch.

"I'm going to ravish you," Mikhail whispers against my neck.

A shudder rips through my body, and I expel a heavy breath, trying not to fall apart.

"Condom?" I ask. Mine are in the bathroom and in my bedroom. I don't leave any lying around in my kitchen. My mistake.

He retrieves one from his wallet while I unbuckle his slacks and undo the zipper. I slide the material down his hips, and he's in nothing but his underwear. He places the condom on the counter, but he doesn't unwrap the foil packet yet.

Mikhail unclasps my bra, taking my breast into his mouth, sucking and licking the peak as his fingers tease me against my panties.

"You're already slick for me," he murmurs, pleased with his accomplishments. He grabs my hips and turns me around, bending me forward against the kitchen table.

Mikhail pulls my panties to the side and swipes a finger along my slit. "That's my girl, nice and wet for me."

I inhale a sharp breath. "Condom," I say.

"Not yet." He smacks my bottom, and I jump before my fingers clench into fists.

"Did you like that?" he asks.

I'm afraid to admit that I did.

"Answer me," he whispers into my ear, and another shiver courses through my body. When I don't answer him quickly enough, he paints my bottom again with his hand.

"Yes," I gasp.

"I can tell you're so fucking wet for me," he says and lets his fingers explore my folds. He touches me, bringing me closer, but not quite over the edge.

He stops long enough to rip open the condom packet and secure it over his cock before plunging into me. Mikhail forces my chest down against the table, pushing my back, holding me how he wants me.

I'm his to do with as he pleases.

He pounds into me.

He's not the least bit slow or gentle.

This is for his pleasure, and I don't mind because it feels good.

I moan and clench onto him as he thrusts into my tight, throbbing core. I'm close, but not quite there.

I reach around, trying to touch my clit, wanting to get off with him, when he grabs my wrists and pins me against the wooden table. "Did I tell you that you could do that?"

He's rough and forceful, and his command makes my insides quiver.

"No," I whisper, even more turned on by his authority.

"You don't touch yourself when I'm fucking you."

I whimper, but it's more because I'm desperate and needy and so fucking close that he's depriving me of the one thing I want right now: an orgasm.

I shouldn't be doing this with him. There are other ways to get close to a suspect other than fucking them, but it's a little too late to backtrack, and besides, I want this.

It feels good. He feels fucking amazing.

"Are you going to let me come?" I ask.

He releases his grip from my hands, and he reaches down between my legs. I inhale a sharp breath, the anticipation overwhelming. He pinches my clit, and I exhale a sharp gasp when he smacks it.

"Do not come!" he commands.

My insides quiver, and I'm teetering on the edge. My toes curl, and I'm gasping and clenching, and he pulls out, depriving me of my final release.

"Fuck!" I curse angrily that he got me so close to the edge and then backed off.

He snickers, laughing, proud of himself. Mikhail lifts me to my feet and turns me around to face him. "You're mine," he says, grabbing me by the jaw, his tongue tracing my bottom lip. "I will be the only one bringing you heightened pleasure."

I whimper in protest. My knees are like jelly, and he props me up so that I may sit at the edge of the table. "Spread your legs," he orders.

I do as he instructs, and he slides between my thighs, his cock hard and thick as he enters me in one swift movement.

My fingers grip his shoulder, and I lie back, bending my legs as he pounds into me. The sensation builds, and the throbbing intensifies with each thrust.

I slam my eyes shut, and my fingernails rake over his back and down to his ass, pulling him closer, deeper, tighter. I want every inch of him.

"I want to come," I whisper, praying that he's heard me and willing to oblige.

My back arches, and my toes curl as I teeter close to the edge. I'm not ready for him to pull out, to withdraw, and leave me trembling and wanting more.

I clench down hard, keeping him locked tight inside of me, holding him against my body as the first wave nears.

"I want to feel you come on my cock," he growls into my ear.

His movements quicken, and he drives deeper inside of my warmth, stretching and filling me.

Fireworks explode in the darkness as I tremble. My hold on him intensifies as I pull him closer against my body. "Mikhail," I breathe into his ear, my teeth tugging the lobe, wanting him to join me.

And he does.

He grunts, and his breathing intensifies, gasping for air as he spills himself inside of me.

He withdraws, taking the condom off and disposing of it in the trash. I climb off the counter and reach for my clothes on the floor.

"Leave it," he commands.

"You want me to leave my clothes off?"

"You can put an apron on, but nothing else."

I chuckle under my breath. "I don't have any aprons," I say. I hold out my hand as he gathers his clothes. "How about I wear your shirt while I cook us dinner?"

He hands over his white dress shirt. It was crisp and clean. Now, it's wrinkled, but it still has all its buttons. I slip it on, and he pulls me close, his hands around my hips. "Leave it unbuttoned," he says. "You look sexy wearing nothing but my shirt."

I'm confident that I'm blushing at his remark. I turn toward the stove, turning the water to boil noodles back on and starting from scratch with the sauce.

Mikhail pulls his boxers on and retrieves his phone, glancing at the device. He exhales a soft huff.

"Is something wrong?" I ask.

"Just work," he mutters and runs a hand through his hair.

He's rugged and rough. The tattoos that cover his arms aren't the only marks on his skin. There are scars on his chest and back. I recognize a few as gunshot wounds, and I imagine the others are stab wounds of some sort.

"The same work where you got those scars?" I ask, gesturing toward his chest. "Is what you do dangerous?" Of course, what he does is dangerous. It's also highly illegal. I don't expect him to divulge all his secrets, but it wouldn't seem natural if I didn't ask.

Any sane woman sleeping with a man who has a dozen scars is bound to ask something.

His answer is gruff and short. "I got them in war," Mikhail says.

"Oh." I exhale a soft breath. "I didn't realize that you were in the military."

He doesn't answer me, and I decide that I'm done pushing the questions, at least for now. I need to get information out of him, but he doesn't seem to want to discuss it.

"I need to take this call. Do you mind if I go to the other room?"

"Sure, you can use my bedroom if you want some privacy," I say.

"Thanks."

It isn't difficult for him to figure out which room is my bedroom. This is a one-bedroom, single-family bungalow. It's cute and cozy, but not practical for a family. It's perfect for me and my cover story.

Mikhail heads out of the kitchen, down the hallway, and I can hear him briefly until he shuts the bedroom door.

While I can't hear a word that's being discussed, my team will have his entire conversation recorded and accessible to them on the cloud server.

I just hope for my sake he doesn't brag to one of his men that he just got laid.

There's a sharp knock on the front door. I turn the water on the stove down. It's not quite boiling yet, and I don't want it to boil over while I'm away from the kitchen.

No one knows I live here. Whoever's at the door can't be for me. It's probably some kid selling cookies or a neighbor introducing themself.

I glance through the peephole and groan.

Aaron Moore is standing on the opposite side of the door.

I pull the door slightly ajar. "Now isn't a good time," I say.

"Were you planning on telling me you moved?"

I scoff under my breath and consider slipping outside onto the front porch when I realize I'm wearing nothing but Mikhail's dress shirt. I pinch it shut with my hand to keep Aaron from getting an eyeful.

"You followed me home."

I'm quite surprised that Mikhail failed to notice the tail on him, but Aaron is incredibly good at not being seen. If he watched me pull up in the driveway, then he saw that I had company over.

"I didn't know you were seeing someone," Aaron says. "You could have just told me. I'd have backed off."

I don't believe him. "Really? Because here you are, bothering me again. It's not bad enough you came to my work, but now you're showing up at my house!"

Mikhail clears his throat from behind me, and I jump. I didn't hear him exit the bedroom or come up behind me at the front door.

How much of the conversation did he hear?

Mikhail grabs my arm and pulls me back, away from the door. "You heard Madisyn. Get off her property, or I'll forcibly remove your ass," Mikhail says. His Russian accent is thick, and his words are gruff.

I swallow the lump in my throat. Does Aaron recognize Mikhail?

Aaron hasn't previously worked with the transnational organized crime division. His division specializes in white-collar crime and handles a multitude of fraud-related cases and investigations.

Mikhail shuts the door and locks it. He folds his arms across his chest. While he's wearing his boxers, he's not wearing anything else, and he is stunning.

"Does your ex-boyfriend bother you often?" Mikhail asks.

I open my mouth to say that he's not my ex-boyfriend, and it's a lot more complicated, but I don't want to give Mikhail any more information than he needs to know. If Mikhail finds out Aaron is FBI, I don't want it coming back to him that I'm also an agent with the bureau.

"He showed up at work today," I say, careful with my choice of words. "I told him to leave me alone."

"Clearly, he doesn't know how to listen, *Kisa*," Mikhail says and exhales a sigh. "I'll make sure he won't ever bother you again."

CHAPTER SIX

MIKHAIL

"I DIDN'T THINK you were coming home tonight," Nikita says. A wide smirk adorns his face.

I glance at my watch as I shuck my coat.

Shit.

I forgot about the flash drive in my pocket. I dig my fingers into my wool coat, but it's not there.

It's not on the floor in the foyer. Did it fall out while I was over Madisyn's? If I'm lucky, it's in one of the vehicles we use.

I run a hand through my hair. I'm exhausted. It's well past midnight. There was no way I was spending the night at her place. She's cute and feisty, but I'd never sleep, and I have a meeting in the early morning. Besides, I can't sleep in anyone else's bed.

I'm always on guard and on high alert when my men aren't nearby.

Too much adrenaline runs through my veins, and now having misplaced the thumb drive isn't helping matters.

I sent Luka to stay outside her house in his car. I need to make sure that she's safe and that asshole of an ex-boyfriend doesn't come back to bother her.

I want to wipe that smug grin right off. He doesn't know anything. It's all assumptions, and even though I did sleep with her, it's none of his damn business.

"I want everything on Madisyn's ex-boyfriend, Aaron."

"Do you have a last name?" Nikita asks.

"Try social media." A growl escapes the back of my throat. "I didn't get his last name when I was kicking him off her property. He showed up at her work, and he's been harassing her. I want one of our men keeping an eye on her at all times."

"You want to give her a bodyguard?"

"Luka is my eyes for tonight," I say and attempt to stifle a yawn. "But yes, until the threat to her is neutralized, she gets a bodyguard."

Nikita opens his mouth and shuts it.

A scowl crosses my face. I don't like it when my men have something to say but refrain from doing so. "What is it?" I'm not in the mood for him questioning my decisions.

"You don't think it's a waste of manpower, having one of our men on her?" Nikita asks.

"What I think is that you need to let me be in charge, and you need to focus on finding out everything about her ex-boyfriend."

"Yes, boss," Nikita says.

"And let me know if you find that silver thumb drive with a red X on the bottom. Last I saw it, I put it in my coat pocket."

Nikita knows what's on the drive. He was part of the team who helped me recover the device and put a bullet in the son of a bitch's head who betrayed me, Leo Aminoff.

Leo stole valuable intel about our safe houses and our guard shifts. He was stupid enough to put an ad on the dark web, attempting to sell the information to the highest bidder.

Dmitri noticed the advertisement, and we set up our little sting operation to retrieve the drive and put an end to Leo's involvement in selling our secrets.

At least the information is encrypted, but it's still worrisome that it could be out there, waiting to fall into the wrong hands.

"Of course, sir." He heads down the hallway in the opposite direction as I head up the stairwell for my bedroom. It's late, and knowing that Madisyn is safe at home, I can shut my eyes and get a few hours of sleep.

———

My phone jolts me awake. "Hello?" I rub the sleep from my eyes and try to focus on the caller. I didn't glance at the caller ID when I answered the phone.

"Boss, you asked me to drop her off at work. I did that, but she just bolted out the front door not five minutes later."

My brain is in a haze. "Luka?" I ask.

Who else would be talking about some girl? I sent him to watch Madisyn last night.

The morning light spills in through a break in the curtains. I sit up in bed, the sheets fall around my waist, and I try to focus a little more on the call.

"Yes, do you want me to follow her or just let her be? I dropped her off at her job, but she isn't inside the building."

My gaze tightens. Where the hell is she heading?

"Follow her, but be discreet," I say. "I don't want her knowing that she's being watched."

I end the call and fall back into bed. As I stare up at the ceiling, the sun is still much too bright. I shade my face with my arm.

Where the hell is my *Kisa* going?

What trouble is she getting herself into?

There's a sharp knock on my bedroom door.

"What?" I shout into the void. I want to be left alone to sleep. But it doesn't seem like that's happening this morning.

"Should I come back later?" Nikita asks through the closed bedroom door.

I grumble under my breath and relent. "Come in," I say.

Nikita turns the handle to my bedroom door and steps inside. He closes the door behind himself. He glances at me, careful not to remark that I'm still in bed at this hour. It's not that late, just past seven in the morning, but I'm usually up, running business decisions and working.

"I ran the information that you requested on Madisyn's ex-boyfriend."

"And?" I ask, waiting for him to answer.

He's stalling and uncomfortable, bringing me whatever details he's uncovered.

"Out with it!" I do not like to be kept waiting.

"His name is Aaron Moore. He's a Fed, works for the FBI," Nikita says.

I expel a heavy breath and sit up in bed. "Is that so?" I say. "And Madisyn Taylor? How do they know one another?"

"Other than from fucking?" Nikita shrugs. "Can't tell. There's no proof of any sort of relationship between them. Which makes it even more puzzling, sir."

"Why is that?" I ask. I push myself out of bed and stand, heading for the dresser. I need to shower and dress, get ready to face the day. Whatever it brings.

"Well, usually when you have any sort of relationship with the person, there are receipts, text messages, photographs, evidence on social media," Nikita says. "However, all that is usually hidden when it's an affair with a married person."

"And is one of them married?" I ask. He ought to know that answer, with me asking him to dig around.

"No, there is no evidence that Madisyn or Aaron have ever been married to anyone else, or each other, for that matter."

I grab my clothes from the dresser and stride into the bathroom, turning around to face Nikita. He's not coming in here, and I'm done with the discussion. "Well, they met. Figure it out!"

I slam the bathroom door shut and shed my clothes, turning the spray on. I need to rinse myself from the thoughts Nikita put into my head.

Aaron Moore is a federal agent. He didn't indicate that he recognized me last night, but that doesn't mean anything. He could be good at his job, hiding his surprise, especially if he wasn't surprised.

Could Madisyn have been a plant? Is it possible that she made some poor decisions, and the Feds have something on her? Are they using her to get to me?

Could she have snatched the drive while I let her borrow my coat?

No, that isn't possible. I searched her thoroughly.

I step under the steaming hot spray and let the last of those troubling thoughts swirl down the drain.

No federal agent would be stupid enough to show up while I'm in her house.

It's a coincidence, one that makes me sick to my stomach. I don't like that she's been screwing a man of the law, and even worse, he's her ex and doesn't seem to take a hint to leave her alone. They did not seem cozy.

I slam my fist into the shower wall. My knuckles burn from the pain. I want to scream at the top of my lungs, but it would only concern my men, and I don't need them running into the bathroom thinking our compound has been breached.

After my shower, I dress and grab my phone. There are no missed calls or texts from Luka. However, it hasn't been that long since I sent him to watch Madisyn.

What is she up to?

Is she meeting her ex? Could she have betrayed me?

I hurry down the stairs and bolt into the kitchen for a cup of coffee.

Dmitri is pouring himself a cup at the coffee pot when I step into the kitchen. He grabs a second mug from the counter, anticipating why I'm here.

"Any news on the cartel?" I ask. I gave him an order to execute Carlos Sanchez.

Dmitri is undertaking the project, and I need to be kept informed, especially if it involves going to war with them. While I wasn't made available last night, I'm here now.

"Aside from Carlos running guns and drugs?" Dmitri pours me a cup and hands it to me before taking a sip from his steaming mug.

"Anything new," I say.

"I've got men watching their rotation, taking notes on their supply runs. We know of one associate whom they've tried to steal business from."

"A supplier," I say, stroking my beard. That's not new information. "What else have you got?" I need more than just bits and pieces. I didn't offer Dmitri the position of underboss so that he could sit on his ass all day.

"I've got men watching Carlos' top-level officials. They're not making a move without us seeing it."

"I pay you to do more than watching the cartel." I slam my coffee cup down on the counter. The hot contents splatters on my hand, but I ignore the searing pain.

Dmitri takes a tentative step back. His eyes are wide, and he straightens his posture. "I assure you that we are doing everything to track down Carlos Sanchez. He's gone dark."

My nostrils flare as I inhale a heavy breath through my nose. "Someone must have informed him that my men are coming to execute him."

It can't be a coincidence that Carlos is no longer in sight. He's probably stowed away at a safe house. I doubt that he's in protective custody. He's not a man to make a deal.

We share that in common.

"I can assure you that it wasn't any of your men," Dmitri says.

I reach for my coffee and take a sip. The porcelain is hot and slightly wet from the earlier spill. "How can you be certain?"

My cell phone buzzes in my pocket. "We're not done with this conversation," I say and grab my phone. "Mikhail," I answer. I take the phone and my mug of coffee out of the kitchen and to my office.

"I've got eyes on your girl, but she spotted me," Luka says.

I exhale a heavy sigh and place my mug on my desk. "How bad is it?" I ask.

"She wants to talk to you."

CHAPTER SEVEN

MADISYN

EARLIER THAT MORNING...

I don't dare admit that I enjoyed last night with Mikhail, but what happened was purely professional. I had to sleep with him to get close, to earn his trust.

But just thinking about him makes my insides warm.

No.

He's a monster. I can't let him get inside my head.

I shower, dress, and head outside to grab the newspaper in the driveway when I spot a dark four-door vehicle parked in front of the house.

The gentleman behind the wheel is familiar. He's the same man who drove the SUV when Mikhail was a passenger on that rainy night.

"Luka," I whisper, remembering his name.

I stalk up to his car. He's not the least bit inconspicuous. I lean forward toward the passenger window, and he rolls it down.

"What are you doing?" I ask.

"Giving you a lift?" Luka offers a warm, friendly smile. It doesn't fit his personality. He's lying. I can see through the charade; it doesn't take an FBI agent to notice his answer is bullshit.

I don't believe him. "How long have you been outside?"

"Long enough to make sure that ex-boyfriend of yours doesn't pay you another visit."

I pinch the bridge of my nose. "Is that what this is about? Mikhail is jealous?"

"No, Mikhail wants to ensure that you're safe. He doesn't trust him," Luka says. He's more forthright than I thought he'd be. "He didn't like that Aaron showed up at your house after you specifically told the gentleman to leave you alone."

"Mikhail told you all that?"

Luka gives a weak nod. "I'm just looking out for you. I can give you a ride into work this morning."

I glance back at my house. "Yeah, give me ten minutes."

————

Luka drops me off at work, and I head inside the building to use the bathroom on the main floor before heading back out the double doors for the coffee shop.

I'm not going there solely for the coffee. It's one of the meeting places to exchange information with my contact, Special Agent Savannah Blakely.

I pull my coat tight and hurry down the street. The quicker I make it inside, the warmer I'll be. I head inside the coffee shop and brush right past Agent Blakely. I head down the hallway and around toward the back of the building. I sneak into the supply room and around the back through a hidden door that takes me into another part of the building, hidden away.

Two minutes later, Agent Blakely joins me.

"I wasn't sure you were coming," Savannah says. Her long blonde hair is pristine, even with the wind and cold. It's any wonder how she looks like a fricking model. She could have easily gone undercover and stolen Mikhail's attention.

"Well, here I am. I made contact with Mikhail Barinov last night. He was at my house," I say, foregoing the details about us in the kitchen. "He made a private call while in my bedroom. You might want to pull surveillance to see who he was contacting."

"Already on it."

"And what the hell is going on with Aaron?" I ask.

"What do you mean?" Savannah is one of the few people who know Aaron and I slept together. It's not that I want it to be common knowledge, I don't, but she warned me it could ruin my career.

"He showed up twice yesterday, once at my job and again at my new house."

Savannah's eyes widen as she realizes the implication. "He's following you."

"He must be. He doesn't seem to realize my assignment, and I'm not comfortable telling him if he's not part of the inner circle," I say.

Her blue eyes wince, and her gaze tightens. "I'll speak with Barrett about Aaron's behavior."

I exhale a heavy sigh. "I don't want to make things worse." I throw my head back and groan. "If Mikhail discovers that Aaron is FBI, it could ruin the entire investigation."

"Forget about ruining the investigation. It could get you killed." Savannah steps closer. "I'm worried about you staying undercover. I think you should be pulled before it gets any more complicated. We can find someone else and start from scratch on earning the bratva's trust."

"No!" I should be grateful that Savannah is trying to protect me. She's a good agent, one of the best, but I don't want to be pulled off the assignment and reassigned to another investigation, or worse, forced to watch another agent interact with Mikhail.

Savannah raises an eyebrow. "No?"

I expel a heavy sigh and try to compose my thoughts. "I've already gained Mikhail's trust. Throwing that all away is pointless. Let me do my job. Just keep Aaron far away from Mikhail and the bratva."

"We've got word that the cartel is stealing from the bratva. Have you heard anything?"

I haven't gotten any information about their business arrangements. "No, Mikhail and I don't talk business," I say. "He doesn't trust me with that type of information."

There's a noise on the opposite side of the door, and we both fall silent. Someone is in the stock room.

Whether they're an employee or someone who doesn't belong, we remain quiet until we're confident that we're alone and no one is listening.

Savannah's voice drops to hardly above a whisper. "You're not part of his inner circle yet, but he will bring you in. It's inevitable."

"What makes you think that?" I ask.

Savannah shakes her head. She won't talk about it. Whether she believes someone is listening in or the fact that we're out of time, I have to head back into the coffee shop.

"Stay safe," she says.

I wait a moment, listening on the opposite side of the storage room door.

Silence.

I sneak into the supply room, but I'm alone. I shut the door behind myself and slip out the main door and down the hallway. I step into line, ordering myself a cup of coffee. I may as well since I'm here.

Stepping up to the counter, I feel a set of eyes on me from across the room. Luka is seated in a corner booth, his gaze locked on me.

Is he following me?

The barista hands me my cup the moment after I pay for it. They're quick today.

I don't want him to notice Savannah, not that I expect he'll know who she is, but it's better to keep his attention focused entirely on me. I block his view of the hallway and tower over him.

"What are you doing here? Are you following me?"

Luka smiles and shrugs his shoulders. He isn't saying anything.

"Did Mikhail put you up to this? To spy on me?"

Luka's gaze is locked on mine, which is a relief. I spot Savannah heading through the main entrance and out the door.

"I'm just here for a cup of coffee," Luka says.

I glance down at the small table in front of him. It's empty of any coffee. There's no tea and not even a cup of water.

"You're full of shit. Call Mikhail. Put him on the phone."

He leans back in the booth, quite pleased with himself and not the least bit intimidated by me. "Mikhail is a busy man. He doesn't have time for your childish games," Luka says.

"My games? You're the one following me into the coffee shop." I try to keep my voice down and not let anyone overhear us, but it's difficult not to make a scene in front of him. I hold the cup of coffee in my hand, trying not to squeeze the top off and spill it out of frustration.

Luka retrieves his phone from his coat pocket. "Fine, I'll give him a call, but he isn't going to be happy to hear from me."

"I imagine not when you tell him that I caught you spying on my ass."

He dials Mikhail. At least, I assume that's who he's calling. He waits a moment before speaking into the phone. "I've got eyes on your girl, but she spotted me," Luka says.

I hold out my hand, gesturing that I want the phone.

"She wants to talk to you," Luka says and hands over his device.

"What the hell are you doing having me followed?" I don't even attempt to keep my voice down. I can feel several sets of eyes staring at me because I'm interrupting their morning coffee break. Well, too bad.

Mikhail clears his throat. "Luka was just trying to make sure that ex-boyfriend of yours leaves you alone."

"I don't need a bodyguard," I say, staring at Luka while speaking to Mikhail over the phone.

Luka winces and shrugs, like maybe I do. How much does this guy know about Aaron?

"I disagree," Mikhail says. "We can discuss it tonight at my house after you get off work."

I wasn't expecting such a forward invitation. "You want to see me tonight?" I was worried he might have lost interest after we slept together and he jetted out.

"Do you already have plans?" Mikhail asks. There's a hint of annoyance in his tone.

"I do," I say. It's a lie. He can't think that I don't have a life, that I don't have friends, or at least work colleagues to grab drinks with now and again.

"Cancel them," Mikhail says. He's short and abrupt. There's no room for discussion. "You're coming over after work."

He's demanding, a definite red flag if I've ever seen one, but I'm not thinking about dating the guy. This is undercover work, and I have to do whatever is necessary to get close with him.

"You won't get sick of me?" I ask and give a weak, nervous laugh. I'm not the least bit uneasy, but I'm playing it up, especially with Luka watching my every move.

There is no one I can trust within the bratva organization.

"Luka will drive you to my place when you're finished with work. Until then, he has orders to protect you."

"That's one way of putting it," I mutter into the phone.

"What's that?" Mikhail asks.

I'm uncertain whether he heard my remark or is pretending that he didn't. "I'll give you back to Luka," I say and shove his cell phone back into his palm.

I don't wait to hear another word from Mikhail, and I certainly don't wait for Luka. I hurry out the door of the coffee shop. It's not like Luka doesn't already know where I'm heading.

———

"Where's my coffee?" Hannah asks as I finish the last sip of my drink and toss the empty container into the trashcan.

"Back at the coffee shop," I say and point behind me toward the elevator doors.

Hannah chuckles and nudges my shoulder. "Next time, buy me one. I'll pay you back."

"Right. Sorry, I didn't even think about it." I hurry down the hallway to change into my scrubs.

She follows behind me, already dressed but seeming to want the company or to talk. I can't tell which. It's not like we don't have a massive case load, but Hannah is the social butterfly around here and an opportunity to strike up a conversation, she'll take.

"You seem distracted. Is everything okay?" Hannah asks.

I exhale a heavy sigh. What can I share with Hannah? Anything I tell her could easily be repeated, and letting her know I'm FBI is absolutely out of the question.

"I started seeing this guy," I say. I open my locker and pull out my scrubs.

She folds her arms across her chest, and her eyes widen. "Go on." She wants details.

I dress as quickly as possible. The faster I'm done, the less story I have to tell.

"My car broke down, the short version, he let me stay over, and now we're... well, I don't know what we are, but we slept together."

"Is that the guy who showed up downstairs yesterday after work?"

"No, that's my ex-boyfriend. Another disaster I'm dealing with around here," I say. I finish getting dressed and slip on my shoes.

"Well, I'll keep an eye out for the ex. If I see him, I won't let him anywhere near you." Hannah holds up her arms like she's going into a boxing ring to protect me.

I quirk a grin. "Thanks." Grabbing my badge, I secure it onto my scrubs.

"You have a new patient in 218," Hannah says. Her complexion is ghastly. There's something behind her eyes. Is it fear? "I'm sorry." Her words are barely above a whisper, but I hear them as she dashes down the opposite end of the hallway.

"I don't understand," I mutter under my breath.

Why is she apologizing?

As I approach the nurses' station, room 218 is just across the hall. I get a nice look at the burly gentleman in his suave suit and hair with a little too much gel, which looks a bit crunchy.

He's standing guard outside of 218.

His arms are folded across his chest, his eyes tight as his gaze follows me as I stalk past the room.

Why is there a bodyguard? The man's not Russian and certainly not one of Mikhail's, but I recognize him.

He's Colombian and with the Sanchez Cartel, Enrique Sanchez.

Luckily, we haven't crossed paths before. I hurry past the guard and saunter around the nurses' station behind the desk to review the chart and information on our new patient, Victor Hernandez, in the computer system.

Carlos recently underwent surgery after taking four bullet wounds to the chest.

Ouch.

Who shot him?

Is that why he has a bodyguard stationed outside of his room? It's not an officer or anyone with the concierge's security team monitoring the patient.

I glance up inconspicuously at the gentleman standing guard. He's one of the dozens of men being investigated for money laundering and drug trafficking.

I don't recognize the patient's name, which means it's not their leader, Carlos Sanchez, or any of their higher-ups.

It's no secret that the cartel has expanded throughout the city and has been hostile to the bratva.

Did the bratva do this? Put this man in our care with four bullet wounds in the chest. It's any wonder he's still alive.

I head toward the patient's room, but Enrique stops me before I can step foot inside.

"I need to check on the patient," I say, pointing at the door. "Are you going to let me through, or do I need to call security and have you removed?"

Enrique steps aside and lets me through before blocking the entrance to the door again.

It's no wonder Hannah was apologetic about me having to deal with the cartel. Did she know it's the cartel, or was she just worried because the guy standing outside the hospital room entrance looks intimidating?

Victor is asleep when I enter his room. I tap the keyboard on the workstation in his room and open his electronic medical records to mark his vitals. I go through the motions, blood pressure, pulsometer, temperature, and he opens his eyes.

They're glassy and red. "I'll be done soon," I say. "Can I get you anything?"

His gaze moves down on my scrubs. "Where's the short skirt?" he asks. "I thought nurses wear those sexy little uniforms to make the patients feel better."

If I wasn't undercover, I'd slug the bastard. "This is my uniform," I seethe. I don't even fake a smile.

His hand reaches out, and I move out of his reach before he can cop a feel. I jot down his vitals and lock the workstation before leaving the room.

The muscle outside the door steps aside.

Two other nurses give me apologetic looks for having to deal with Victor.

Do they realize he's with the cartel or just feel bad that I'm the new girl and I get the patients they don't want to deal with?

I grab Hannah's arm and pull her into another hallway, out of sight of the bodyguard. "How often does the cartel bring their men here for care?"

"They're cartel?" Hannah's eyes widen. "I thought he was just some scumbag drug dealer from a gang. It's the first time I've seen him, but the bodyguard, he's practically a regular. Maybe once every few months, they bring in someone who's been shot or stabbed and needs surgery. We all draw straws to decide who gets to deal with them."

"And I'm the new nurse on the unit, so I got picked?" I'm not the least bit offended. I deal with thugs and thieves often enough in my line of work. Smiling weakly at Hannah, I don't want her to think I'm upset with her. "It's fine. I can handle him."

"The bodyguard or the patient?" Hannah asks. She gives a nervous laugh and fiddles with her hands in front of her.

"Both. I've encountered my fair share of ogres."

She chuckles, and the tension eases out of her shoulders. "Okay, good."

As it nears lunch, I head down to the cafeteria to grab a quick bite to eat.

Stepping off the elevator, two men are arguing. One of them is Mikhail Barinov. The other is Carlos Sanchez.

The cartel and the bratva.

I skirt past the commotion and head into the cafeteria, out of sight. I'm not sure, but Mikhail may have spotted me. Even so, I'm not getting in the middle of two men butting heads and throwing threats at one another.

The two men stir quite a commotion, bringing in several onlookers, and finally, I hear the heavy boots of security forcing the two men to break up the exchange.

I pay for my food and grab a seat at a nearby table. I can see the chaos through the glass window. There aren't very many open options for available seating, and while I'd rather hide in a corner and not be seen, the only chance I have to do that is to take my food upstairs to the unit.

"Madisyn!" Mikhail shouts my name as the security guards intervene.

His gaze is deadlocked on me.

Even if I wanted to hide, where would I go? Under the table?

I exhale a heavy sigh and stand, leaving my tray of food unattended while I step out of the cafeteria into the hallway where the two men are bickering.

Victor is being escorted out the front door.

Mikhail doesn't seem to be as agreeable with leaving.

"Sir, we're going to have to ask you to leave," the security officer says.

"Madisyn! She can vouch for me," Mikhail says.

I step around into the hallway, wishing that I could be invisible.

No such luck.

"Do you know this gentleman?" the security guard asks.

Mikhail's eyes are franticly searching mine, silently begging me for my help.

"Unfortunately, I do. "

CHAPTER EIGHT

MIKHAIL

I DIDN'T INTEND to involve Madisyn, but the two-bit security for the concierge doesn't know who I am. I should have his job for trying to force me to leave.

I'm part owner of this establishment, not just a client.

It's why I'm fuming that Carlos Sanchez shows up for medical attention. There are other hospitals, clinics, physicians he could see elsewhere.

He doesn't get to tramp on my turf because it's convenient for him.

"Can you tell him that he needs to leave, or we'll have to contact the police?" the security guard says to Madisyn.

She's in her scrubs, her hair slightly disheveled, and she looks exhausted.

Is that my fault? Was she not able to fall back asleep after I left?

"Come on, I'll walk you outside," Madisyn says.

I'm not sure why I thought that she'd stand up to the security guard and tell the bastard to leave me alone, that I'm with her. That was naïve. This isn't her fight. Hell, she doesn't even know or understand why I'm arguing with Carlos Sanchez.

I shrug out of the guard's grasp and accompany Madisyn out the front door. The security guard is watching the entire time. She doesn't need to come out into the cold, and she's shivering as the automatic doors open and a rush of cold air whips into the atrium.

"Do you want to tell me what is going on?" Madisyn asks.

It's not a surprise that she has a lot of questions, and I want to talk to her, but I need to know that I can trust her, that she's loyal and has my back.

"Other than that man doesn't belong here?"

She offers a weak smile as she steps outside beside me. "Are you okay?"

It's freezing. The sun is high overhead, but I can see my breath with every exhale I take.

Madisyn must be chilly. She wraps her arms around herself and bounces from one leg to the other to keep warm.

I don't need her catching a cold because of me.

"Go back inside before you get sick." I shove my hands into my coat pockets.

"I don't know what's going on, but you need to leave before that guard calls the cops," Madisyn says and glances over her shoulder.

The security guard is still standing in the hallway, watching the exchange between us. Not that he can hear a word of what we're saying, but he's probably making sure that I'm leaving. He has a walkie-talkie in his hand, and I'm confident if I don't keep moving, he's going to bring in the local police.

I don't need any more drama or trouble.

There's no sign of Carlos outside. He probably already caught a ride and left.

"Fine, I'll go. But Carlos has no business being here. I don't want him setting foot inside that building again."

I'm part-owner of the establishment. Don't I get a say in who we let in through the front door?

"Just deal with it another day. Okay?" Madisyn says. "Whatever is going on, take a walk, chill out."

"I can't. One of my men was shot because of that bastard, Carlos." I've tried to keep my temper in check and handle this professionally. I showed up at the concierge center, looking for Madisyn.

I wasn't expecting to find the cartel hanging out downstairs in the lobby.

There was a firefight between my men and the cartel. I never considered that we'd both show up at the same location to seek treatment.

Going to the hospital is out of the question. One of our guards at the front gate, Ivan, was shot when the cartel threatened our home.

They never made it inside. It was a warning because we've been closing in on Carlos. He sent his low-level thugs to exact revenge.

"I need you to come back with me."

"What? Now?" Madisyn glances behind her at the building. "I have to be back upstairs in twenty minutes."

Traffic will take us at least that long to get to the compound, not to mention the time it will take to stitch up Ivan.

"Come with me." It's not an offer. It's an order. I grab her arm and bring her toward the awaiting SUV. The vehicle is parked by the front entrance.

Ivan is lying in the back seat. I wanted to bring him in for treatment, but if the cartel is hanging around the medical center, then it isn't safe for him.

"Get in," I say. I have my gun on me, and I could threaten her with it if she doesn't obey.

She senses my urgency and climbs into the back seat.

"He needs to go inside for treatment," Madisyn says as she climbs onto the bench seat beside him.

"Not with the cartel hanging around. I went in to grab a wheelchair to lug his sorry ass inside, but I ran into Carlos instead."

I climb into the front seat.

The engine is on. The vehicle is already warm.

I hit the gas, and we jolt forward. I can't sit around waiting for security or the cops to show up, not with Ivan already losing a lot of blood in the back seat.

"Where are you taking us?" Madisyn asks.

"The compound," I say and glance in the rearview mirror. There's no sign of Carlos or the cartel.

She exhales a heavy sigh. "Take off your coat."

"What?" I ask, glancing back at her.

"I need to stop the bleeding. I'm not taking off my blouse. I don't have anything on underneath. Give me your coat," Madisyn says. The girl is practically ordering me around, but I do as she asks.

I shrug out of it while driving, no easy task, and shove it back at her between the two seats. "Here."

I'd ask her not to get blood on it, but since I think she's about to shove it against his wound to stop the bleeding, I guess I'm out eight hundred for a suit coat.

"Let me take him inside the clinic," Madisyn says. "If it's about the guard—"

"This has nothing to do with that stupid guard," I mutter.

Traffic is grid-locked ahead. I make a sharp right, and Ivan groans from the pain, or maybe it's the sudden intense turn that doesn't help.

"Can you drive a little more recklessly?" Madisyn shouts at me.

"Traffic was stopped. I'm trying to get us there quickly and in one piece." Maybe I should have left her ass at work and picked up a different nurse, someone nicer.

I hit the gas harder, weave in and out of back roads, and blow through two traffic lights just as they're turning red then fly by a stop sign.

I'm keeping an eye out for any cops, but I'm in a hurry.

"How's he doing back there?" I ask.

"He's lost a lot of blood. His pulse is dropping. I need you to turn us around and take us back to the concierge center."

I huff under my breath. "No chance of that happening. Not while the cartel is waiting for us to show up."

"The cartel wasn't waiting for you," Madisyn says. She's a little too quick with her answer.

"What do you mean?" I growl.

What does she know that she isn't telling me?

"One of my patients seems like he's probably with the cartel," Madisyn says. "He had a bodyguard outside of his room."

"What's his name?" I'd stop the SUV and interrogate Madisyn, but every second could mean life or death for Ivan.

My soldier in the back seat is breathing shallowly, and the groaning and wincing in agony are diminishing.

"I can't tell you that, and this isn't the time, Mikhail," she shoots at me. She's pissed.

Maybe I deserve it. Then again, I'm still on fire from finding out her ex-boyfriend is a federal agent. I sure as hell don't need him sniffing around.

"Keep him alive, *Kisa*. Your life depends on it."

"My life?" Madisyn asks, her voice growing louder. "I left work early and will probably get fired for helping you out. So, yeah, that seems fair, threatening my life when all I'm doing is helping you."

She's cheeky. I'll give her that.

"Really? That's all you're doing? You're not working with your ex-boyfriend to get dirt on me?"

I glance up in the rearview, pinning her with my stare.

Her brow is furrowed, and as soon as we lock our gazes, she shakes her head and returns her focus and attention entirely to Ivan.

Good, she needs to keep him alive.

I don't want to have to kill her. It'd be a real shame.

"I found out your ex is a Fed. As in Special Agent of the FBI," I say.

She hasn't returned my stare—her focus on Ivan.

I glance back at the road, where I need to be paying attention. Another sharp right and I've rerouted us around the traffic jam.

"Yeah, so what? It's just his job. Why does it matter?" Madisyn asks.

I clear my throat. When she puts it like that, I feel like an ass.

I haven't told her that I'm bratva or that my business associates are my blood brothers.

I don't want to be in bed with someone who might be spilling my secrets to the enemy.

"I don't like cops sniffing around my property," I say. I have to ask, even though I don't want to give her a heads up that it's missing. "Did you steal something of mine?"

"Of course not! What are you talking about? What could I have possibly stolen?"

I don't answer her question. I turn back to the conversation about Aaron. "Are you and he friends? I don't like how he showed up last night."

"Did it look like we were friends last night when he came to my house, bothering me?" Madisyn snaps.

She's got a point. And that's why I had Luka keep a close eye on her, assigning her a bodyguard in case he shows up again. Though at the time, it was more about protecting her, now I need Luka watching her make sure she's not divulging anything to him.

Even more so now that I'm bringing her in to help Ivan; she's going to see things that she can't unsee.

We pull up outside the gate. One of my men lets us in and shuts the metal contraption behind us. I park in front of the main entrance and shut off the engine.

The front door opens. The attendant must have notified my men at the gate. Nikita and Dimitri hurry outside and open the back door, helping carry Ivan inside. He's slumped forward, and each man puts an arm around his shoulder as they maneuver him up the main steps and into the compound while trying to hold the bloody jacket in place to keep him from bleeding out.

Ivan is pale. He's always been a bit fair-skinned, but he looks ghastly. Perspiration appears across his brow as my men lug his ass inside.

I toss my keys at Luka as he follows outside. "Park it for me," I say.

Madisyn climbs out of the back seat after Ivan is lugged out by two of my men. "You're coming inside with me," I say and gesture for her to follow.

She's right on my heel.

Her hands are bloody, the scrubs marked with crimson, stained from helping one of my men.

She'll need a change of clothes and a shower, but not before fixing up Ivan. She's got work to do.

Madisyn follows close behind me. She's inside and accompanying me down the hall where my men have taken Ivan.

"You're going to need supplies," I say and lead her toward a storage supply closet.

I open the closet door and ignore the look on her face. She's surprised that I'm prepared. She wouldn't be shocked if she knew this wasn't our first rodeo. Knife fights and bullet wounds are unfortunate side effects of the job.

There are more than just basic supplies in the closet. I've got everything from a medical-grade skin staple to suture needles. There are plenty of gauzes, rubbing alcohol, an assortment of illicit and prescription drugs, and I.V. equipment for minor surgery.

Two years ago, I lost a man because I didn't have the right equipment. It's why I partnered with Steele Concierge Medical. It was supposed to make things easier. They don't ask questions or involve the police. But the cartel wasn't supposed to be there, either.

It was exclusively our facility, along with a few billionaires and wealthy businessmen who wanted the perks of a concierge center.

It was never supposed to be open to the public. Why the hell was Carlos hanging out in the lobby? If his men required medical attention, they could go to the hospital.

Madisyn had mentioned that one of his associates had been on her unit.

Who?

Ivan had shot some bastard who had attacked him, but by the time my men made it out to back his ass up, the cartel had driven off.

———

"You did a good job," I say as she finishes the last of the stitches on Ivan's abdomen after removing the bullets.

"He's going to need to rest, and he really should get some antibiotics to make sure that his wounds don't get infected."

"You tell me what he needs, and I'll get it for him," I say.

He's not going to a hospital, and we're certainly not going to Steele until the cartel is gone.

"I don't have my prescription pad," she says.

I didn't realize she was a nurse practitioner and could prescribe medication. Keeping her around would be handy.

Although I'd never really asked either precisely what she does for a living.

"It's fine. Just write down what he needs. I'll handle the rest," I say. I give her a pad of paper, and she jots down the medications and dosages.

After she's written down the information, I hand it over to Dmitri. "Deal with this," I say.

"That's how you handle things?" Madisyn asks. "You have your men do it for you?"

"I delegate orders to men I trust." I glance her up and down.

She's covered in dried blood. Even with the gloves that she'd used while operating on him, she still had blood on her clothes and had handled him in the back of the SUV.

"Come with me."

She follows, but she's not the least bit quiet. "Where are we going?"

"You need a shower. You're covered in blood, and I need to dispose of your clothes." There's no chance the amount of blood that's burned onto her scrubs will come out. "Shoes off," I instruct before we travel up the staircase.

She slips off her black shoes. They're at least passable. The black hides any blood, but that doesn't mean there isn't evidence left on her.

"I'll have them taken care of," I say. "Come with me."
I lead her up the stairwell and to my bedroom. She
will share my private bathroom.

I open the bedroom door, flip on the light, and lead
her inside, shutting and locking it behind her.

"Strip."

"Excuse me?"

"You need to shower, and I need to dispose of your
clothes. Everything off." I gesture to hurry up.

"Fine." She heads for the bathroom, but I block her
from closing the door. "What do you think you're
doing? This isn't a free show."

"See, but it is," I say, tilting my head and staring at
her. "You're going to strip down, step into the shower,
and bathe. And I'm going to watch you."

"Excuse me?" Her mouth hangs open.

Good.

"I don't need you keeping any bit of evidence of what
happened tonight. I need to make sure it's all gone.
Destroyed or down the drain. Now strip."

"I'm not getting naked for you," Madisyn snarls at me.

I laugh under my breath. "That's not what you said last night."

Her eyes narrow, and she yanks the bloodied top up and over her head, tossing it at my face. "You're an asshole."

"That may be, but you still fucked me. You found something irresistible about this asshole." I smirk, enjoying the show.

She's riled up and on fire. "Oh, there's plenty to resist now that I see you for what you really are!" Madisyn pushes her scrub bottoms off and throws them at me.

I catch her pants this time, holding them scrunched up in my hands along with her top. "Panties too," I say and gesture with two fingers for her to give them to me.

"Why? They don't have any blood on them."

"No, but they're mine."

She rolls her eyes, pushes them down in haste, and slingshots them at my face. I catch the black lace pair of panties and bring them to my nose. In doing so, I feel their dampness on the cotton.

"You're turned on right now."

I should have seen it, the stance, her dark gaze, red, rosy cheeks.

"Bra too, and the socks have to go."

She unclasps her bra and then slips off one sock at a time before shoving the items into my hand. "Are you happy? You forced me to get naked. What kind of a man does that make you?"

"I'm doing it to protect you. How would you explain the blood if someone found it on your scrubs?"

"I work in the medical industry. It wouldn't be the first-time blood or vomit has gotten on my clothes."

The amount of blood covering her work clothes wouldn't be something a person could overlook. "Get in the shower."

She steps toward the bathroom shower, pulls back the glass door, and turns on the water. It takes a moment for the temperature to warm up before she steps into the stall. I slide the door shut, the glass giving a hint of her silhouette, but believe it or not, I'm not here for the show.

I need to know without a doubt that I can trust her, that there isn't any blood left behind.

Which means a thorough scrubbing. She can't have any evidence under her fingernails or a missed spot on her back.

I should join her.

I strip out of my clothes. My shirt has blood stained on the collar and sleeve but isn't nearly as noticeable as Madisyn's clothes.

My pants probably have blood, but the black makes it difficult to see. I'll burn my suit along with her clothes—no sense in risking evidence of the attack.

As bratva, we always have to take precautions.

"I'm coming in with you," I warn her as I open the shower door.

"What?" Her eyes are shut, and her head is dipped back under the spray. Water falls over her, cascading down her naked skin. She looks irresistible.

"I need to make sure you get all the blood off, and I could use a shower too," I say.

Her eyes open, and she glances me up and down. "Lame excuse. If you wanted to shower with me, all you had to do was say so."

My top lip snarls as I playfully growl at her, grabbing Madisyn by the waist pulling her against me. "I need to make sure you're clean. Every inch of you."

I lean closer, my lips teasing hers but not quite kissing her. The shower's steam mixes with the heat and passion fueling between us.

"Are you going to clean the filth right off of me?" she asks.

"If I have to scrub it all off, I will," I whisper. I brush my lips against hers and tug on her bottom lip, bringing it between my teeth.

She whimpers and trembles in my arms.

The water is clear. Most of the blood that caked her skin has swirled down the drain before I stepped foot into the shower with her.

I grab her jaw, turning her head slightly from side to side. I like holding her, controlling her, but I'm also examining her porcelain skin to make sure there aren't any remnants of blood. "I can't have you with so much as a speck of blood on your skin."

"Why?" she whispers, staring up at me through heavy-lidded eyes.

Is she really asking me that?

"Your little ex-boyfriend would love to—" I stop myself from further elaborating.

"Would love to what?" Madisyn asks. Her head is tilted to the side, my hand on her jaw, and I let go.

He'd love to get me behind bars.

"It doesn't matter," I say. It's not as though the blood is from a murder that I committed. We were attacked, but the police and the Feds aren't our friends. They're not to be trusted. Not now and certainly not ever.

They can twist stories around, and I don't trust that they wouldn't use Madisyn against me, especially that scum-sucking ex-boyfriend of hers.

Hastily, I turn her around to face the shower spray, pushing her up against the shower stall.

Her hand braces the ivory tile as water drips down every inch of her naked skin. She's glistening and sexy. I want to hear her scream my name in ecstasy.

My mouth brushes against her ear.

She shudders in my embrace. "Tell me you want this," I whisper.

"I want you," Madisyn answers. She turns her head to the side and squirms in my grasp, attempting to turn around.

I don't let her.

"And you will have me, but know that you've seen too much," I say, warning her of the danger of what she's gotten herself involved in with our messes. "There's no going back."

While she might not have been given a choice, she's in deep, and there is no escaping the dark underworld.

"I wouldn't want to," she says.

Her words are like a symphony. My fingers tangle in her long tresses, pulling her hair to one side on her shoulder, tugging a fistful of her vanilla locks.

"You're mine, *Kisa*. You belong to the bratva and to me."

I seal her fate with a fiery kiss.

She doesn't back down or pull away. There's no fighting her fate. She succumbs to it like she's meant to be here, meant to be under me.

I don't typically allow women in my ranks to work beneath me. They tend to complicate matters, or rather, relationships do, but there's no turning back. She's seen the blood of one of my men spilled and helped patch him up.

There were no questions, no blatant curiosity. She obeyed like a good little girl, and I will reward her.

My fingers tease her breast and slide down across her stomach.

She rests one hand against the shower wall, and with the other, she grasps at my hip from behind herself. Her movements are rough, and her nails scrape over my skin. She's searching for me, silently begging me to fuck her.

And I will, *Kisa*. All in due time.

"Swear to me that you're loyal." I nip at her neck, leaving a mark against her collarbone. She's mine, and I want everyone to know that she belongs to me.

Madisyn's voice is hardly above a whisper. It's drowned out by the sound of the shower beating down against my back. "I swear."

I lick along her collarbone, where there's a slight red blemish. My fingers wander over her hip and between her thighs, pushing her legs farther apart.

"Promise me that you're obedient." I want to hear her declaration. I wait to touch her where she craves to feel pleasure until I've heard everything I need to from her lips.

She hangs her head. One arm supports her weight against the shower wall. The other roams through my hair.

She's desperate. I can sense her neediness and her desire for me. "I promise," she says and whimpers.

My fingers tease apart her folds. Already, she's wet for me.

I tangle my fingers in her hair and pull her waist back against mine. "You are mine, *Kisa*." I thrust my cock inside her.

She moans and whimpers as I fill her pussy. I bend her forward and continue thrusting.

One hand grips her hip, the other, her hair, keeping her bent over.

Her insides tighten around my cock, trembling and spasming. I can feel her on the brink.

"Mikhail," she gasps, her breath raspy, tinkering on the edge.

But I don't let her come yet. I'm in control, not her.

I want to fuck her harder, faster, and feel the jolt of power rivet through my body, but not yet.

I shut off the water, satisfied that we're both clean from earlier.

She stands and turns around to face me. Her cheeks are flushed, and she's breathing heavily. "Where are you going?" Madisyn asks.

"Out of the shower," I command.

I don't answer her question. She will obey me like she's promised and be rewarded for her submission.

I slide open the shower door and step out, grabbing a towel and tossing it to her to dry off. I grab one for myself and am quick to wipe down the beads of water coating my skin.

I'm rock hard, and she doesn't fail to notice my desire.

I give her seconds to dry off before I open the door to the bedroom. "Follow me."

She runs the towel over her body. Her hair is dripping wet, and she removes the towel long enough to try to catch some of the water droplets from her curls.

I'm pleased that she isn't fighting me and is doing as I instruct. It's rare to find such a precious gem.

"Climb on the mattress, on your back."

She drops the towel to the floor and does as I say.

My towel joins hers in a heap as I close the distance between us.

"Touch yourself," I say, staring into her dark brown eyes.

"What?" her voice squeaks. There's trepidation behind her gaze.

I stalk closer, climbing onto the mattress on all fours. I don't touch her, just hover above. "I want to watch you pleasure yourself."

Her tongue darts out and swipes across her top lip. "I've never—"

"I don't believe you."

"You didn't let me finish," she says. The blush from earlier has spread across her cheeks and neck. "I've never done that in front of anyone," she says.

"Good," I say and smirk. "I get to be your first."

Pride rises through me. "I'll even let you come if you can bring yourself to do so in front of me."

She rolls her lips together and lets out a nervous laugh. Her fingers trail down between her thighs. She begins to rub along her slit and up to her clit.

I can smell her arousal, and I want to taste her, devour her, and feel her crumble against my lips.

But I make her wait, and it only makes my cock throb harder.

"Tell me what you're doing," I say.

Her voice is hardly above a whisper, and her eyes have shut.

"Touching myself."

"Look at me," I command.

Her eyes lazily open, and her breathing deepens as her fingers glide against her pussy lips. "That's my girl," I say, proud.

I shift down on the bed, watching her ministrations as her pearl swells and she teases the bead.

My cock throbs as I watch, and I imagine she's aching inside, wanting my cock to fill her. "Change hands. I want to taste you," I say.

I move my hand over hers, guiding her fingers into her wetness, coating her digits.

"Mikhail." Her voice is raspy and breathless.

I sense her trepidation. I bring her fingers to my lips, tasting her wetness, her essence, and climb back over her body, teasing her lips.

My fingers stroke her, caressing her lips, teasing her clit. Her hips shift on the mattress as she grows restless.

I hover above her lips and drag my tongue over her top lip and then her bottom.

I glide two digits inside of her warmth, and her wetness seeps out as I fill her.

Madisyn's moans are soft and timid. She doesn't have to be that way with me. I want her to be fearless and confident. "Come for me," I whisper against her ear and gently suck the lobe.

She whimpers and trembles on my two digits. I slide a third inside of her pussy, teasing and finger fucking her.

Her hips rise off the bed, and she's gasping for air. "Fuck me, please."

I could never deprive her of anything, especially when she asks in that desperately needy tone that sends my cock spasming.

I withdraw my digits long enough to stroke my cock with her wetness and glide inside of her warmth.

Her head dips back, and her back arches off the mattress as I fill her.

She leans up, capturing my lips, pushing her tongue inside my mouth, hungry for more.

I want to give her everything, all of me.

Her insides clench onto my cock, trembling and spasming.

"Come for me," I rasp against her lips.

She pulls me deeper, tighter. Madisyn's legs wrap around my waist, and it's like fireworks explode on the darkest night.

My eyes slam shut, grunting as she moans my name into my ear, and I am finally able to let go.

I roll off her body and lie on my back, panting hard. As I stare up at the ceiling, Madisyn comes into view.

She shifts to lie against me, and her hand drapes across my chest.

"You're perfect, *Kisa*."

Her cheeks redden, and she shifts and rests her warm cheek against my chest.

While I want to pull her tight, throw the covers around us, and drift off to sleep, that's not on the agenda.

"That's enough rest," I say and gently push her to sit up in bed.

Madisyn grumbles her discontent.

"I have a surprise for you."

CHAPTER NINE

MY INSIDES STILL throb from the intense orgasm that Mikhail gave me. I can't remember the last time being fucked ever felt so damn good. Except for yesterday, with Mikhail.

My heart won't stop slamming against my ribcage, and Mikhail has another surprise in store for me? I'm not sure how much more I can take.

"A surprise?" I sit up in bed and want to reach for the covers, but they're buried under the pillows. The bed is still neatly made, almost pristine except for the wrinkles we've made.

He grunts as he climbs off the mattress.

I can't take my eyes off his physique. He's got a dynamite body, thick and muscular. Not to mention his strength.

"This is for you," he says and approaches his dresser. There's a large white box, and he brings it to the bed. "Open it."

I have no idea what he could have gotten for me.

The box is plain and simple. It does not indicate its contents other than its size is quite large. He's certainly not keeping a ring or a pair of earrings inside.

I lift the lid and pull back the crisp, white tissue paper folded around a black gown. It shimmers in the light and is gorgeous.

"I want you to wear this for me tonight when we go out," Mikhail says.

"You're taking me out?" I'm surprised that he's interested in having me accompany him anywhere. "Is there a work function you have to attend?" I ask.

I don't recall any upcoming soirees for the bratva, but that doesn't mean there isn't one happening. I just might not have been brought in on the event because my team wasn't made aware of it.

"I'm taking you to dinner," Mikhail says.

————

"This place is amazing," I say as I sit across from Mikhail. We're given a table in one of the most ostentatious restaurants in the city. "How were you able to get reservations?"

"I'm a partner in the establishment," Mikhail says. "The chef and I are friends. He wanted a restaurant but didn't have the funds. I wanted a restaurant but didn't have a chef."

I can't tell if he's joking or if there's more to the story. I wasn't aware that he was part-owner of any restaurants. What else don't I know?

"That's kind of you, helping a friend out," I say. I give him a genuine smile. I'm impressed he has more ventures than just the illegal kind, although he could be laundering money through this place. It's something to further investigate and report to Savannah when I contact her.

Mikhail reaches for his red wine and swirls the glass, breathing in the aroma before tasting. "It's not all generosity."

I smile politely, like I don't understand what he's trying to say. "What do you mean?"

"I'm a businessman, and I only take risks that guarantee my success."

"But how could you know that this restaurant would be a success?" I ask. "Nothing in life is guaranteed." I reach for my wine and take a taste. It's sweet, fruity, and quite perfect, with no overpowering acidity or aftertaste. It is the best wine that I've ever tasted.

It also wasn't on the menu.

Mikhail asked for it specially. Just like our meals.

"Consider it a calculated risk, one that is very low," Mikhail answers. He's cryptic and careful not to give anything away that I could use against him.

Not that he has an inkling that I'm FBI. If he did, he wouldn't have slept with me. Hell, I probably shouldn't have slept with him, but going deep undercover means doing whatever is necessary to get the job done.

And it wasn't like I didn't want to sleep with him. I'd do it all over, again and again.

"Madisyn!" Thomas Slate, one of my colleagues from Quantico, strides right up to our table. He's in a black suit and tie. Coming to this place, means he's either on a fancy date or schmoozing with one of the bosses.

Mikhail clears his throat, his gaze hardening. He doesn't appear the least bit pleased that a gentleman recognizes me.

"I haven't seen you since our Qua—"

I interrupt him before he can say another word. "It's been too long," I say and force a smile. "Thomas, this is Mikhail." I introduce them, but am careful not to use the word boyfriend regarding Mikhail. I'm not sure what we are. Even undercover, we haven't quite established our relationship.

"I'm Madisyn's partner," Mikhail interjects.

"Oh," Thomas says, his eyes widening. Does he think we're FBI partners?

My stomach is doing somersaults. I have to stop him before he says anything that could get either one of us killed.

"It was nice to see you again. It looks like your date is waiting for you," I say and point toward the front entrance, giving him a hint to leave.

Thomas swiftly takes it, glancing at the door. Whether he's with a date or not, he seems to get the message. "It was wonderful seeing you again, Madisyn. And it's nice to meet you, Mikhail. Take good care of her."

"I wouldn't dream of anything less," Mikhail says. His eyes are tight as he studies my expression and then Thomas as he heads out of the restaurant.

The moment Thomas exits the front door, Mikhail is on me with his interrogation. "What was that about?"

"What?" I ask innocently. "Thomas? He's just an old friend." I don't want him getting jealous. I don't know what he'd do to Thomas if he felt threatened in any way.

Mikhail lifts his wine glass. He doesn't take a sip yet. His gaze is locked on me. "How do you and Thomas know one another?"

It feels a hundred degrees and like I'm under a heat lamp. "We met in college," I say, coming up with an excuse. "We were on the same floor in the dorm."

"Co-ed," he says. He swirls the wine around in the glass before indulging with a taste.

"That's right. We were just friends. We had a couple of classes together."

"And where did you go to school?" he asks. His gaze tightens.

"Columbia University, in New York."

Mikhail places his wine glass back onto the table. "I thought you were from Ohio?"

"I grew up in Ohio. My family lives there, but I went to school in New York. That's why I came back here, looking for a job."

"To be with Thomas?"

"What? No!" I laugh at his absurd thought process. "I came back here because I had lived in New York in college and loved the atmosphere of the city. It's quite different from Cleveland." I sip my wine, pinning him with my stare. "I never took you for the jealous type."

Mikhail straightens his shoulders and clears his throat. "Who said anything about being jealous?"

"It's written all over your face, your body language, even the questions that you're asking me."

I take a deep breath. I need to settle down. Fighting with Mikhail isn't going to help my assignment. I have to get close to him, and if I push him away, I'm only hurting myself and the investigation. Hell, I'll be letting down my team.

I should be relieved that dinner is brought out, but instead, there is mounting tension between us.

He barely looks at me during dinner. Like I've betrayed him. He has no idea what I've done, who I am.

There's a heaviness between us, and halfway through our meal, his steak knife in his hand, he pins me with his stare. "Are you with the FBI, Madisyn?"

My mouth is dry.

Thomas blew my cover.

I swallow back my nerves. "No," I say, my gaze meeting his. I don't waver or cower. I refuse to blink.

"I don't believe you." Mikhail doesn't put down the knife.

He wouldn't use that here, in a public place, would he?

He hasn't physically threatened me yet, but I'm terrified of what he will do if I can't convince him that he's wrong.

"Why would you think I'm working with the FBI, Mikhail? You've seen me at the medical center. I'm a nurse. I bandaged up your friend. You came to my work and picked me up during the day. Do you think if I was with the FBI, I'd be hanging around a concierge medical center?"

He exhales a soft puff of air, but his expression is unconvinced. "Why did it sound like your old buddy, Thomas, was about to say that he knew you from Quantico?"

"You're mistaken," I say. "He was saying that he knew me from Columbia. He didn't finish his sentence. Both sound similar."

"No, they don't." Mikhail's gaze never leaves mine. "It's not a coincidence that your ex-boyfriend works at the FBI."

I can't deny that Aaron is a Senior Special Agent in white-collar crime.

"That's all it is, Mikhail. A coincidence."

Mikhail gestures to the waitress that we're done. There's no bill to pay, a benefit of being part owner in the establishment.

He's ready to leave, and I doubt he'll let me go home or walk free.

I'm as good as dead if he believes that I've betrayed him.

"I don't believe in coincidences, *Kisa*. I was naïve about your ex-boyfriend. I looked the other way because I liked you, and I made a mistake."

He accompanies me outside, his hand wrapped around my waist. There's no chance of me running. I can feel his gun against my lower back as we approach his car.

"Get in," he commands.

"I'm not your enemy," I say.

It's the truth, but will he believe me?

He opens the back door and yanks me around, grabbing my hands behind my back. He binds them with a zip tie from the glove compartment before he pushes me into the vehicle.

He's not the least bit warm or gentle. However, I've never known Mikhail to be either of those traits. He's firm, and while he's been fair and reasonable toward me, I doubt I will have the benefit of those attributes to experience tonight.

I'm shoved into the vehicle, and he slams the door shut. He hurries around to the driver's seat and starts the engine, pulling away from the restaurant.

He hits the gas hard, and I fall back against the seat.

I shift forward and inconspicuously lift my arms, trying to slam my wrists down and apart to break free from the plastic binds.

I had plenty of training years ago at Quantico to escape from zip ties, but I wasn't situated in the back of an SUV and trying to break free without being noticed.

Mikhail's gaze shoots up at me every so often.

I'm lucky he didn't shove me into the trunk. If he catches me trying to escape, he'll put a bullet into my head.

We drive past his home. Mikhail doesn't so much as slow down.

"Where are you taking me?" I ask.

He's heading toward my house or the highway. Both are in the same direction, and if he gets on the highway, I'm good as dead.

No one will find my body. No one will ever know what happened to me.

Mikhail doesn't answer.

But I breathe a sigh of relief when he pulls up out front of my home. Maybe he'll leave me here, tell me never to contact him again, and we'll part ways.

Could I be that lucky?

He kills the engine and steps out.

Mikhail waits a moment outside of the vehicle. He's on his phone, texting someone. Is he trying to get information on me?

Shit.

I turn sideways in my seat, staring out the window at him as I attempt to break free of the zip ties. I lift my arms as high as possible and swing downward and out, breaking the bindings.

It burns, but it's worth it.

Mikhail shoves his phone into his pocket and opens the back door before I have time to react.

He grabs me by the arm and forcefully escorts me to my front door. "I see someone figured their way out of the restraints." His top lip snarls like he's disgusted with me. "Key." He says it like it's a command.

"It's in my purse," I say, the small handbag in my grasp.

He yanks it from me, unzips the leather, and fiddles through until he's satisfied before shoving it back at me.

"You find it," he grunts.

Was he looking for my key or searching for a weapon in my purse?

It's dark outside, but I'm able to find my key without too much difficulty. I unlock the front door and push the door open.

Mikhail is on my heel. He nudges me inside and follows.

Is this where the FBI is going to find my dead body? At least I have a gun hidden inside my apartment. But it's in my bedroom. There is surveillance equipment, but I doubt the FBI is watching my every move, especially at this late hour.

"What are we doing here, Mikhail?" I ask, turning to face him. I place my purse on the counter and slip out of my shoes.

"I need to know that I can trust you, and I don't think I can," he says. He steps closer, invading my personal space.

I should back away, cower.

But I don't. I stare up into his unwavering gaze. His hands are bunched into fists, and he's fuming. "You betrayed me!"

"I don't know what you're talking about," I say. "I work for Steele Concierge Medical."

He snorts. "Yeah, that's what you want me to believe. I have my men doing another background check on you. Digging deeper into your past." He waves his gun at me. "Sit on the sofa."

"Mikhail—"

He cuts me off before saying anything further and shoves me backward onto the couch. "I said sit," he barks.

"I'm not one of your men you can order around."

He huffs under his breath. "No, you're right. My men are worth more to me than you are, little girl."

"I'm not a little girl!" I snarl at him and jump to my feet, darting toward the door.

He grabs me by the waist.

"Get off me!" I shout and shrug out of his grasp, stepping on his toe and kneeing him in the groin.

Mikhail growls at me. "That's enough!" He lifts his gun to my forehead. "Don't give me another reason. You're already on borrowed time."

"So, you're going to kill me?" I should be afraid. Any sane person would be quivering and begging for their life.

"I ought to," Mikhail says and pushes me to sit back down on the couch.

When I oblige, he lowers his gun to his side. It's still in his grip. I could disarm him, but he could also shoot me in my attempt. He's well-trained and not just any thug with a gun.

He's bratva.

He's a ruthless monster. I was warned to tread carefully, get him to trust me, and not get too close.

Sleeping with him wasn't part of the plan, and there is no way I can tell my colleagues what we did. Not if I want to keep my job when this is over and done with. That's assuming I'm still alive and Mikhail hasn't killed me himself or ordered a hit on my head.

"But you won't?" There's a sliver of hope strumming through my chest. "You care about me," I say.

"I don't care about a rat."

I haven't told the FBI anything. At least not yet. I haven't betrayed his trust, aside from masking the truth and lying about who I am.

But he won't see it like that. Do I come clean? Do I tell him the truth?

He'll probably kill me, but maybe I deserve it.

"You're right. I work for the FBI," I say.

CHAPTER TEN

MIKHAIL

MADISYN BETRAYED ME. The little bitch made me believe that she was a nurse. Maybe she is, but she's also a conniving Fed.

I can't trust her.

I shouldn't even let her live. She knows too much. She's a liability to the bratva.

"Don't move," I snarl at her while she's sitting on the sofa. Her hands are clasped in front of herself.

"Are you going to kill me?" Madisyn asks.

Her voice is soft, tentative. It's a trick. She's trying to make me feel something for her.

All she makes me feel is cold and lifeless.

I'm disgusted with myself for trusting her. She's a stranger, and I blindly let her into my home. I trusted her, and that's my burden to bear.

"Seems like an easy solution to a difficult problem," I mutter.

The truth is that I don't want to kill her, but she did lie to me. But I don't know why. Is she working for the Feds undercover to take me down? Or is she a forensic nurse? Maybe something in between, and we just happened to cross paths.

No.

She's not innocent.

I don't believe that we just happened to meet.

"Did your car even break down?" I'm sure it did. She was driving a piece of junk. I glance around the house. It's bare, impersonal. "This isn't your home." It's an observation, not a question.

She doesn't answer me.

Madisyn is afraid of me. She's staring up at me. Her bottom lip quivers, but she bites down. She's trying to hide her fear.

She ought to fear me. I could bury her alive, and no one would ever find her body.

She's silent. She probably realizes that anything she says will further incriminate herself and give me more ammunition. Not that I need any more.

I have enough to hang her.

"Why?" I ask. I wave my gun at her, demanding answers.

She exhales a soft breath. "Why do you think? You're bratva."

"You're a shitty agent." I want to hurt her. It starts with biting insults. I'm biding time, waiting to hear from my men. And before I kill her, I need to know what information she passed on and what dies with her.

She presses her lips together and folds her arms across her chest. "I had you fooled. You thought I was in love with you."

Her remark is intended to burn, but I know better. I lean closer, invading her personal space. "You were begging me with your wet pussy to fuck you."

She shifts on the sofa, scooting farther back and away, toward the corner to keep her distance. "And you couldn't tell if a woman faked it or not."

"You're a shitty liar." There's no way in hell she was faking an orgasm. I'd bet my own life.

"Me? You thought you could trust me," Madisyn says. "I wormed my way into your home and your bed. I'm not as shitty as you think."

My hands bunch into fists, and she covers her face.

She's afraid of me.

I should revel in the thrill that I've broken her. But instead, it burns my insides like a fierce inferno.

The doorbell rings.

It's probably one of her Fed friends checking up on her. Or maybe that ex-boyfriend. Was he her ex, or was that a ruse?

I glance out the window and recognize the vehicle out front. It's that stupid ex-boyfriend.

"Answer it," I say, waving my gun at her. "But no funny business." I gesture for her to walk to the door.

She exhales a shaky breath and climbs off the sofa.

"Madisyn, it's me. Open up." Aaron's voice is muffled but still clear enough to decipher his words through the door.

I stand behind the door, gun in my hand. "Get rid of him," I whisper. "But I swear, if you do anything to indicate that I'm here, you're both dead."

"I won't," she says softly before unlocking the door. She only opens it a few inches. "Now isn't a good time, Aaron."

"Let me in," Aaron says. "I know he's here. His vehicle is outside."

This asshole isn't going to leave, is he?

I yank open the door and flash my gun at him. "Get inside!" I bark orders.

Aaron throws his arms into the air. "Hey, no one needs to get hurt. I'm just here to talk."

"Talk?" This isn't a hostage negotiation. There's no talking that needs to be done. Not with him. He's one of the enemies. "Get inside."

He keeps his hands up, and Madisyn takes a step back, letting him into the house.

I shut the door with my foot and pat him down, making sure Aaron isn't wearing a weapon.

"Lock the front door." I give Madisyn orders. "Close the blinds," I instruct, in case there are other federal agents nearby.

She obediently follows my instruction. Is it because I'm waving a gun? It's certainly not because she's loyal to me.

I glance at Aaron and Madisyn.

I did not start tonight intending to take hostages. But that's what this shit has turned into.

Fuck me.

I don't need two dead federal agents and their bosses sniffing at my door. This is a job that I'd typically delegate to Dmitri or Nikita. But I'm on my own tonight.

I did this to myself, but I'm not going to end up six feet under.

Aaron strides across the living room, standing in front of Madisyn. I'm not sure if he thinks he's protecting her or just wants to get his grimy paws on her.

"You don't honestly love this guy?" Aaron jabs his thumb in my direction. "You know he's bratva, right?"

I'm not sure if he's truly as clueless as he's claiming to be or trying to save Madisyn from me.

I click off the safety on my gun, pointing it at Aaron's head.

"Wait!" Madisyn lunges between Aaron and my gun.

Does she believe that I won't shoot her? Because it wouldn't take much to pull the trigger.

Sweat glistens on her forehead. And she's breathing heavily.

She's nervous.

"You're protecting him?" I can't quite wrap my head around why she'd willingly take a bullet for the greasy-haired agent.

Is she still in love with him?

My finger itches on the trigger. A pang of jealousy hits me like a stab wound to my gut.

"Please, don't do this, Mikhail." Her voice is soft and comforting. Her gaze never wavers. Her words pull me from my reverie. "The FBI has nothing on you. You're a free man. If you kill Aaron, they'll lock you away forever."

I'm not the least bit afraid of a prison sentence. I've already been through one trial and gotten off.

"Isn't that what you want? Me behind bars." Why else would she have infiltrated my family?

Madisyn exhales a heavy sigh, and her eyes linger on my lips before moving up to meet my stare. "You've done nothing wrong. If you kill Aaron or me, everything changes."

She isn't wrong.

Madisyn has nothing on me. The FBI's investigation is worthless. I'm confident that I haven't given her any bread crumbs to use against my men or me. And if she had possession of the flash drive, it would all be over.

She lifts her hand, and her fingers graze my cheek.

I want to kiss her, devour her, push her down on the bed, and show her who's fucking in charge.

She leans in on her tiptoes and brushes her lips against mine. She has a calming effect on me, like a drug that messes with my head.

My grip remains firm on the gun, but as I kiss her, I latch the safety, letting the weapon fall to my hip.

I deepen the kiss, biting her lip, and hearing her whimper stirs my cock. I want to fuck her, and I'd love to make the asshole behind me watch.

"Please, I know you're not a monster. Somewhere, deep inside of you, you care about me. And I'm going to say that I still think you do. Or you'd have killed both of us already."

She's trying to connect with me, and I get it. This is her way of pleading for her life. She's not a woman to get down on her hands and knees and beg for forgiveness.

Madisyn likes to think of herself as my equal. But she's not.

She's FBI, and we can't be anything more than strangers because of that. We're destined to be enemies.

"Go home," she says, her hand falling to my chest. Her touch is comforting and peaceful. "Before we're at war with one another. Believe it or not, I don't want anything to happen to you."

"We're already at war."

I pull away from her grasp and shoot a look behind her at Aaron. He's lucky that Madisyn kept me from putting a bullet in his head. I stroll toward the door, turn the lock, and yank it open.

I head for my vehicle without a word, leaving Madisyn behind with her ex-boyfriend. Hopefully, he's a better man than I am.

She deserves better, even if I loathe her for her betrayal.

CHAPTER ELEVEN

MADISYN

"WHAT THE HELL WAS THAT?" Aaron is on me the minute I shut the door. I've just secured the lock to make sure Mikhail doesn't change his mind.

Aaron is in my face. He's taller than I am, and while there was an insane chemistry between Mikhail and me, it's unrequited with Aaron.

Or rather, I used to like him before I got to know the real Aaron Moore. The persona at work isn't anything like the man when he leaves the office.

"What?" I try to defuse the situation. I don't want him to know what's happening or harass Mikhail. If I can end what I started, so be it.

"Don't play dumb with me, Madisyn. You're not really a blonde."

"You're such an asshole." I should have shown him out the door with Mikhail.

Mikhail's car door slams shut, and the engine kicks on, roaring as he revs the engine. Any minute he'll be gone, but I'm not sure that I feel any safer. Not while Aaron is still locked inside my house.

"Me? How am I the asshole? I came here to warn you that your new boyfriend is with the bratva. What the hell is going on? Is he an assignment or your new boy toy?"

I take a step back.

"I'm not doing this with you."

The whirl of an engine roars again, and I'm confident that Mikhail just left.

Relief is not what I'm feeling.

Dread lulls in the pit of my stomach.

Hopelessness. Anger. Fear.

Aaron isn't a good guy. Sure, he works for the FBI, but there are plenty of bad agents, just like plenty of bad seeds. I just didn't see it before it was too late.

"You need to leave," I say and head for the front door.

Aaron rushes after me and grabs my arm, his grip strong and forceful as he yanks me around.

I wince from his strength and the mark that he's bound to leave on my arm. "Get off me!" I knock his arm down and push him back, my hands firmly against his chest.

"You want to play rough?" He stalks closer. "Is that why you were dating Mikhail Barinov? Because you like it rough and dirty in the sheets?"

"You don't know what you're talking about." I refuse to tell him anything. It's clear that he's been kept out of the operation and his entire team reassigned. Why is that? What did he do to get his ass in trouble? How is he even still an agent?

"I know that you're just another notch on Barinov's bedpost. You mean nothing to him."

"Get out!" I scream at Aaron and move out of his grasp. I bolt toward the door to show him out, but he's quicker.

It doesn't help that he's taller, making his strides faster. He grabs a fistful of my hair, yanking me toward him.

Aaron leans in close to my ear. "I thought you liked it rough. Isn't that why you're bedding the bratva boss?" He takes a deep breath, inhaling my scent. "Tired of sleeping with your old FBI boss and moving up the ranks?"

"I don't know what I ever saw in you." I slam my heel onto his toes and thrust my elbow backward into his groin. "Get off me and get out of my house."

"No one tells me when to leave." His grip doesn't loosen on my hair, and he slams my face into the door.

"You fucking asshole!"

"No, that's the problem. You're not fucking me. You're sleeping with him." Aaron drops his grip on my hair, and I take a step back, keeping distance between us as I open the front door.

"I can't believe I ever slept with you," I mutter.

"Well, believe it, sweetheart. And believe me when I say this isn't over between us. You'll come crawling back to me when you realize Barinov's too good for you."

Aaron steps outside and onto the porch. The minute he's out the door, I slam it on his ass, ensuring he doesn't come back inside. I don't ever want to see him again, but I'm not that lucky.

———

I don't bother going into Steele Concierge Medical the next morning. What's the point? My cover's been blown.

I pack up my belongings, including the flash drive, and head outside, waiting for a cab. While my cell phone hasn't been replaced since the rainstorm, the landline in the house works. I never thought I'd be grateful to have an accessible landline.

Thunder echoes in the distance, and lightning illuminates the sky. I grab the umbrella and open it as the first droplets of rain come crashing down.

I hurry to the cab and toss my bag into the back seat with me, heading to the FBI headquarters downtown.

The giant pair of sunglasses in a rainstorm looks odd, but I'm trying to mask the black eye that Aaron gave me last night. I tried a bit of concealer, but it wasn't enough to hide the mark left behind.

I can't wear the shades inside the office. It's much too dark. I remove them but keep them in my palm as I step out of the elevator.

I don't want to be here.

I'd rather be cleaning bedpans and taking patients at the medical center. Maybe I should have continued to work there, if only to keep far away from Aaron.

I should have taken the cab to my house, but if there was any chance of being followed, I wanted to come straight to the office. However, I didn't see any sign of Mikhail or his men outside the house.

"Oh my gosh! What happened to you?" Savannah catches sight of me the minute I step out of the elevator. She rushes toward me, a file in her hands, but she opens her arms to hug me. "Are you okay?

Did that bastard Mikhail do this to you? I swear I will kill him myself."

"Long story," I say and exhale a heavy breath. My gaze travels toward Aaron.

He's in his office, a cup of coffee in hand. He strolls out, heading right for Savannah and me. "Morning." He steps closer and leans down, invading my personal space, taking a long look at the mark that he left.

"Ouch. Did your boyfriend do that?"

"I have to speak with Kingston," I say and take a sharp turn, heading down the hallway.

Savannah leaves me in peace. Aaron chases after me.

"Are you planning on telling him about last night?" Aaron asks. He keeps his voice low as he accompanies me down the hallway toward our boss' office. The door reads Supervisory Special Agent Barrett Kingston.

It's closed, but the doors and walls are all made of glass. The window shades are open, and Barrett gestures me to come inside.

"About last night? Are you worried I'm going to tell him that you slammed my face into the front door, and that's why I came in this morning with a black eye?"

Aaron's gaze tightens, and his hands bunch into fists. "You don't want to do that, Madisyn."

"And tell me, why the hell not? I should press charges against you for assault."

He laughs at my threat. "Assault? I was saving your ass from that bratva boyfriend of yours. You do realize associating with known criminals can get you kicked out of the bureau."

"You're such an ass." I'm done talking with him. I pull open the door to Kingston's office and step inside, grateful when Aaron doesn't follow me inside.

"Agent Carter, I'm surprised to see you in the office this morning."

He steps around from his desk and shuts the door behind me.

"Please, have a seat," he says.

I exhale a nervous breath and do as I'm asked. "You have quite the shiner this morning. Is that why you broke your cover and came into the office?"

"I take it no one saw the video recording from last night."

"No, we haven't gone through yesterday's surveillance footage. Is there something that we should be looking for?" Barrett comes around and sits at the edge of his desk. "Perhaps a fight?"

"This isn't from Mikhail," I say, gesturing to my face.

"It isn't?"

I glance toward the window. Aaron is in the hallway talking with James, a field agent.

I've tried to keep what happened between us a secret. I didn't want anyone to think that I'd gotten special treatment from the boss or was trying to climb my way up the ladder.

But it's gone too far.

"How is the undercover operation going?" Kingston asks. He steers the conversation away from my visible bruise and back to the case. "Any new information that we can use on the Barinovs and their organization?"

"The bratva is good at keeping secrets," I say. The flash drive is buried in my coat pocket. I'm not ready to give it up and turn it over to the FBI, at least not yet.

"And you're here now because something happened. Something other than that black eye." Kingston is trying to make sense of why I'm in the office, which is against protocol. He could be yelling at me for showing up, but instead, he's calm, albeit too calm.

"My cover was blown, sir."

"How did that happen?" Barrett asks. He leans forward, his hands on his slacks.

"Someone recognized me from Quantico, another agent." It is when Mikhail realized that I'd been lying to him all along. "We were at dinner, and he came up to the table. I tried to steer the conversation, but Mikhail didn't become the boss by being slow."

Barrett strokes his jaw, interested in the turn of events. "And he let you live?"

"I'm here now," I say. I don't tell him how it was dicey last night, that I thought he'd put a bullet in my head or Aaron's, possibly both of us.

"I'm glad you're safe. I'd like Savannah to debrief you on the mission so that we don't miss any details."

"There wasn't much, sir. I wasn't able to gather any intelligence information. His men were never nearby with any work-related responsibilities. I was kept in the dark."

"How about at that medical center? Anything there?"

"The cartel showed up, and one of their men is on the second floor seeking treatment." That's not anything that the team couldn't have gathered on their own.

"Is the bratva responsible for this occurrence?"

"I have no idea. Mikhail seemed genuinely surprised by the cartel showing up at the medical center." I left out the part where his man was bleeding, and I accompanied him back to his home to patch him up.

Some details aren't entirely necessary.

It's not that I'm trying to protect Mikhail. There's just no reason to delve into what happened. It doesn't affect the case or the investigation.

Okay, maybe I am protecting him a little.

He didn't pull the trigger. He could have killed me. I'm insane for defending him, but he's not nearly as bad as Aaron Moore.

Mikhail never gave me a bruised eye. Not once did he hurt me.

Sometimes the monsters are right in front, hiding, waiting, ready to make their next move. I'm used to demons.

"Anything else?" Barrett asks.

I don't disclose that I slept with Mikhail or have the flash drive in my possession. I should tell them both things. Even though the first could tarnish my reputation, I did it for the job. Right?

It wasn't because I wanted to have sex with Mikhail. I shift uncomfortably.

Just thinking about him fucking me stirs my insides and floods me with warmth.

Is it hot in here?

"I didn't get anything," I say. "He showed me into his home, was kind, and put on a polite front. Maybe he suspected from the beginning that I wasn't to be trusted."

Swear to me that you're loyal.

Mikhail's words replay in my head.

I should betray him. He's the devil.

Barrett nods and stands. "Well, I'll have you go over everything with Savannah. Is there anything else that you'd like to discuss?"

"No, sir."

"Are you sure?" He towers above me. I don't feel threatened by his presence, like when Aaron is in my proximity. With Barrett, it's more like a father staring down at his daughter, waiting for her to spill her secrets.

But mine are locked deep inside where no one can know what happened.

The surveillance footage.

I want to destroy the evidence of the attack.

But I can't.

Just like I can't give up the flash drive.

I'd do anything to protect my reputation, and Mikhail is on that tape too, threatening two FBI agents at gunpoint, but I won't risk prison time for tampering with evidence.

But the thumb drive, no one has to know that I stole it from Mikhail's residence. It will disappear.

———

After going over the specifics of the undercover operation with Savannah, I head to the lab to review the surveillance footage.

It's leverage against Aaron. While I don't want it to come out that we slept together, there may be little choice in the matter.

Aaron is dangerous. He wasn't when we first met, or maybe I was naïve to the dangers. I worked under him, did as he asked, no matter what it entailed. Usually, it was professional requests, but there were times that things got heated and passionate.

He exuded power, and I fell right into his hand.

Never again.

I open the door, and Aaron steps out from the lab. My breath catches in my throat. "Looking for evidence?" he whispers into my ear as he walks by.

"What?"

"The little tiff at the house, it, unfortunately, wasn't recorded."

"You tampered with evidence?" My voice catches in my throat.

He didn't. He wouldn't.

The Department of Justice has its separate investigation department for employees suspected of violating the FBI's standards of conduct, the Office of Professional Responsibility, O.P.R.

I could have used that tape against him, but now it's gone. Without it, it's his word against mine. And he'd probably blame it on Mikhail.

"I didn't do anything," Aaron says, a glint in his eyes. "One of the backup drives failed saving yesterday's data. It's a shame." He stalks past me, beaming with pride.

I want to kill him.

But I'm not a murderer.

I know a man who is, one who's capable of brutality and savagery. But I'm not the kind of person who would call for a hit.

I'm a federal agent.

I'm supposed to be on the right side of the law. But then why does being right feel wrong?

I head out for lunch and am grateful the day is half over, and I can go home tonight to curl up in bed with a good book. I need a night to myself to unwind and relax.

"Do you want company?" Savannah asks as I lock my computer console.

"Sure, if you don't mind going out in the rain."

It's dark outside, the long, picturesque windows make it seem like it's nighttime, but it's because it's storming.

"You don't want to grab something from downstairs?" she suggests.

I don't want to be anywhere near Aaron, but that's not something I'm ready to discuss with Savannah while at work.

"It's just a little rain."

Savannah chuckles. "You're going to get soaked. Bring me back something, anything."

I grab my umbrella and head down to the elevator. The lights flicker, and I grumble. I swear if I get stuck in the elevator instead of getting to enjoy a nice quiet lunch by myself, I'm going to be in a grumpy mood.

I could take the stairs, but I'm hungry, and I want to make it before the lunch crowd shows up. Although with the storm, it's possible it could be quiet.

Thankfully, the elevator doesn't get stuck, and I get the pleasure of getting soaked in the rainstorm.

I hurry with my umbrella outside. It does little to shield me from the torrential downpour. Maybe Savannah was right, and I should have stayed in for lunch. I could have waited until Aaron came back. I doubt that he went out to lunch in this weather.

I hurry down the block, waiting for traffic to clear and the light to change before I can cross the street.

A black SUV stops at the crosswalk, and the window rolls down.

"Get in," Mikhail says.

I'm already soaked. It's reminiscent of the first time I climbed into the vehicle with him. I exhale a breath.

"I think I'll walk. It's a lovely day."

He rolls his eyes at my joke. He's not the least bit amused by my sense of humor.

The vehicle behind him honks its horn when he doesn't turn quickly enough because he's trying to convince me to come with him. I don't know where he's going or what he intends to do to me.

I gesture for him to move on. I'm not getting in, and he's blocking the flow of traffic and pedestrians from crossing.

He closes his window, and the driver slowly lurches forward. The hazard lights flip on, and Mikhail jumps out into the rain.

"See what you made me do?"

"Really? We're doing this now?" I ask. We're just outside the FBI field office. There are cameras everywhere, not that I have anything to hide.

"Who did that to you?" Mikhail asks, staring at my bruise. "Was it that scumbag, Aaron?"

I don't defend Aaron. He did hit me, and he got brutal with me last night. It could have been a whole lot worse, but it stings. "Why do you care?" I ask.

I lift my umbrella higher to shield Mikhail and myself from the storm. It doesn't matter. My clothes are soaked. My hair is wet and clinging to my body. It's chilly, and I'm trying everything.

The only good news is that I have my suitcase from the earlier assignment and all my clothes are inside, upstairs. I can change if I need to.

"We may not be on the same side, but I don't like seeing you hurting," Mikhail says.

"Right, that's why you put a gun to my head." I don't buy his line of crap for a minute.

He shakes his head and glances away. I have the ability to frustrate him, it seems. Good. He tears his gaze back to mine. "You put yourself in front of my gun, *Kisa*, to protect a monster."

I don't defend Aaron. "Maybe you should have shot him," I mutter under my breath. I don't mean it. I shouldn't even say it to a man who kills people for a living.

Does he consider it a sport or a necessity?

I don't ask. I don't want to know how he can steal someone's life and snuff it out.

"Come with me," Mikhail says.

"The FBI knows I've been made," I say. "If I go missing—"

"I'm not going to force you to come with us. If you'd rather get soaked in the rain, be my guest." He stalks back toward the SUV.

I open my mouth. Part of me wants to go with him. I shouldn't want to—he's bad news, and I could end up losing my job by consorting with a criminal.

"This can't happen, Mikhail," I say.

He opens the door to the vehicle. "All I'm offering is a ride."

I don't believe him. It's never that simple, not with Mikhail Barinov, and certainly not with the bratva.

CHAPTER TWELVE

IT TAKES everything inside me not to turn around and drag her into the vehicle. It's pouring outside, Madisyn has a black eye, and I'm not in the mood to play games.

I climb into the passenger side and shut the door.

"Wait a minute," I say, holding up a finger to Luka.

Rain pours down on the windshield. It's difficult to see much of anything, but I have my gaze trained on the side mirror.

She hurries across the street, soaking wet. The umbrella she has is absolute garbage, not even worth bringing out in the rain. She should be inside or taking a cab to wherever she's going.

"Follow her," I say.

Luka glances at me. "I'll obey your orders, but I've been around enough women to know that she doesn't want to be followed."

"What am I supposed to do?"

I don't expect an answer from Luka, but he gives me one, anyway. "Leave her be. I don't know why you're chasing her. She's a Fed and bound to get your ass thrown in lockup."

"Did you see her black eye?"

"Yeah, never took you for one to rough up the ladies," Luka says. He glances at me before flipping on his blinker to pull out into traffic.

"I didn't lay a finger on her."

"Do you know who did?" Luka veers into traffic and hits the gas. We lurch forward abruptly as he cuts off another vehicle.

"Yeah, her ex-boyfriend, Aaron. He's an asshole," I mutter. The seatbelt tightens as Luka is forced to slam on his brakes. Traffic is a nightmare in the city, and the rain isn't doing us any favors.

"Have an address for him?"

"He works with her," I say and pinch the bridge of my nose. I'd like to mess up his face and teach that bastard a lesson. But he's a Fed, which puts me in a predicament. If I rough him up, I'll have to kill him.

"Staking out the Feds and waiting until he gets off work, okay, that's a tough sell. I can't say I'm thrilled with the idea, but you know I never turn down a challenge."

At least he's honest.

"Don't worry. I'm not going to touch him. I won't have to because Madisyn will come crawling back to me."

"And you want her back, boss?" Luka turns the corner, and I realize we've driven in a circle. We're back on the main road, the same one that Madisyn had been walking down earlier.

It is a coincidence that we drove by and saw Madisyn. We hadn't intentionally cruised past Federal Plaza. We were on Lafayette Street heading to a business lunch, which was canceled.

"I don't want Aaron anywhere near her."

"And you are going to accomplish that how? They work together; you said so yourself."

"I'll get his ass fired."

Luka pulls the vehicle over to the side of the road. "You might as well get out here."

He's dropping me off so that I don't get soaked. It's a little late for that, but I open the door and climb out of the SUV. The rain hasn't yet ceased, and while we intended to meet our associate for lunch, it'll just be the two of us.

Luka pulls back into traffic to park the vehicle around the block.

The bell on the door jingles as I open it and step out of the rain. I'm still quite damp from the storm, but I'll survive.

I catch a glimpse of Madisyn, drenched from head to toe. Her hair is dark when wet and tangled. She's soaked as she stands in front of me, waiting for the hostess to seat her for lunch.

She glances over her shoulder and emits a heavy sigh. "Are you following me?" Madisyn asks.

"I'm just here with Luka to grab lunch."

"And he is—" Madisyn glances around the restaurant and then behind me, presumably searching for him.

"He's parking the vehicle," I say.

I wasn't following her, but the idea is tempting, to see where she lives, who she is outside of the persona she pretends to be when she is with me.

Her brow furrows, but she doesn't say anything.

"Table for two?" the hostess asks as she grabs the menus from the counter.

"Just one," Madisyn answers.

I gesture toward her bruised face. "We still need to talk about what he did to you." I don't take kindly to men who beat up on women.

Even though she betrayed me and pretended to be someone she's not, she didn't deserve his wrath.

Only mine.

But I wouldn't hit her.

"Mikhail," Luka says as he shuffles inside out of the rain. The umbrella held up well for him. I should have used that damn thing when I talked to Madisyn earlier in the storm.

We're quickly seated at a table not too far from Madisyn. I have a direct line of sight on her. She glances at the menu briefly before gesturing the waitress over to order.

"I thought it was over between the two of you," Luka says. He lifts the menu and pretends to read it. We've eaten here dozens of times. He always gets the same meal.

"We're not gossiping about my personal life." I throw him a look to shut up.

"It's not gossip if I'm talking to you about it," Luka says. He puts the menu down on the table. "Not that you want my advice, but go talk to her. You've been staring at her since the minute I stepped foot inside, probably longer."

I grunt and glance away from Madisyn. She's been staring at her phone since the waitress left. "I don't want anything to do with her," I say.

"You're a shitty liar."

"That's enough!" I growl at him to shut his trap. This discussion is over.

————

We finish lunch, and it's taken far more energy than it should to ignore Madisyn. When she finally gets up to leave, I breathe a sigh of relief.

She's been a distraction for the entire meal.

We pay the waitress and get up to leave. Madisyn finished a few minutes earlier, and I would have expected her to have walked back.

But it's still raining.

Shit.

She's standing by the door.

"I'm going to use the bathroom real quick," Luka says.

"You can't fucking wait?" I'm already standing, and if I sit back down at the table, it'll look like I'm intentionally avoiding her. Which, at this point, I am.

Luka ignores me and scatters off to the back, where the bathroom is situated. Is he trying to piss me off, because he's doing a grand job at it?

I stalk past several empty tables and make my way to the front entrance.

Madisyn stands by the door, her crappy old cell phone in her hand.

Is she waiting for the rain to pass? It could be hours. The forecast wasn't calling for it to lighten up until tonight. "Do you want a ride?" I ask.

"No, I'm waiting for my rideshare," Madisyn says. She grumbles something unintelligible under her breath.

There's an awkwardness and heaviness felt as we stand just a few feet apart.

"I'll bet your boss was proud of you." It's a cheap shot, but I can't help but feel anger and hatred toward her for what she did.

"Excuse me?" She glances from the glass door to me.

"Being able to infiltrate my organization." I'm careful not to use the actual terminology out in a public setting. "I'll bet they're giving you a medal for that. It couldn't have been easy."

Her eyes tighten, and there's a flicker of something unfamiliar. "Yeah, a real gold star for getting made. I'll go down as the agent who fucked a bratva boss and still didn't get a piece of intelligence to use."

I open my mouth but quickly shut it. Why the hell is she pissed? I didn't betray her. She knew who I was from the beginning.

"That's my ride," she says and breezes out the door.

She climbs into the back seat, and my stomach flops. I catch a glimpse of the driver, Santiago Rodriguez, a runner for the Sanchez Cartel. A lowlife scumbag on the bottom ranks. He's a nobody, but he's loyal to Carlos.

Usually, he runs drugs and guns. I've never known any cartel members to work for a rideshare service, not even on the side.

What the hell is Santiago up to, and why is Madisyn going with him?

She's already out the door and in the back seat of the sedan by the time I step out into the rain. The vehicle pulls away from the curb and merges with traffic.

Madisyn has no idea what she's done and who she's with. But I don't have the keys or know where Luka parked the vehicle to chase after her.

"You ready to go?" Luka steps outside and opens the umbrella, shielding himself and me from the rain.

"The cartel just grabbed Madisyn," I say.

"What do you mean grabbed?" He points in the direction that we should head to retrieve the vehicle. I could wait inside. Usually, I do, but this is more urgent than usual.

"Well, she went with them. But she has no idea that it's Santiago from the Sanchez Cartel. She thought she was taking a rideshare vehicle back to the office."

"And you would know that because?" Luka asks.

We turn the corner and head into the parking garage. Luka closes the umbrella, carrying it with him as we head to the stairs. "It's one flight," he says.

We walk up the stairwell. It's faster than waiting for the elevator, and at the moment, I'm in a rush to find Madisyn.

"I talked to her before the car pulled up. I didn't see who the driver was until just before they left."

I want to be wrong, but it was Santiago who I saw driving the car.

Luka opens the door to the second floor and leads me to the vehicle. "What do you want to do, boss?"

"Let's start with trying to find them and track them down," I say. "They have a few minutes head start, but you know how traffic is. Hopefully, they haven't gotten far."

CHAPTER THIRTEEN

MADISYN

"WE JUST PASSED the turn for the address that I gave you."

I double-checked the license plate and the vehicle's make and model before climbing into the back seat.

The driver doesn't answer.

"Sir?"

We slow down as we come to a traffic light, and I yank the door handle, but it doesn't budge.

Shit!

I always check to ensure the child safety lock isn't latched when I get in the back of a rideshare vehicle.

But I'd been so focused on Mikhail and trying to ignore him during lunch that I'd been distracted.

"Who are you? What do you want?" I try not to let my voice quiver, but I might not get another opportunity if I don't fight now.

He's silent.

Does he work for Mikhail? Is he going to threaten me because I betrayed his family?

Maybe it has nothing to do with Mikhail. I certainly don't recognize him as a member of the bratva.

Does he have a vendetta with the FBI?

Or maybe he's just a pervert who wants to get me alone.

It doesn't matter, and I need to get out while I still can. We're not far from the office. I can see the skyscraper from the road. We're a block away but heading in the wrong direction.

I don't have much but my hands and my purse. I don't have my weapon with me because I'd been undercover. It's locked up in my safe at home. Little good that is doing me right now.

I grab the straps for my purse and yank it around the driver's neck, cutting off his oxygen supply, choking him.

He slams into the vehicle in front of us, and I'm tossed around the back seat.

"You bitch!" he snarls and yanks the steering wheel hard as he slams on the gas, moving around the car that he just hit.

He weaves between vehicles and recklessly crosses traffic, driving on the wrong side of the road before he veers off into an alley.

At the opposite end of the narrow road, is a black SUV.

The driver slows to a crawl before cutting the engine.

Two men in dark suits step out from the vehicle blocking the road. The rain has lightened up, but neither seems to care about getting wet.

I don't recognize the taller and more muscular, bald man who was driving, but the second, who comes around from the passenger side, he's familiar.

He's an associate of Mikhail's, more specifically, an errand boy.

"Sergei?"

Why are they doing this?

The tall bald associate yanks open the back door and reaches into the vehicle, grabbing my arm.

"Mikhail sent you?" I can't believe the nerve of him and pretending like he gave a damn about me!

"Come with us," the bald man says. He doesn't answer my question. He drags me toward the awaiting vehicle while Sergei quietly says something to the driver.

I can't hear what's being said, and I don't care.

"Get off me!" I scream, fighting back. My elbow hits the guy in the ribs, but he doesn't so much as flinch.

We're in a darkened alley. There are no witnesses, no windows, no sign of anyone but us.

If I go with these men, I may not have another opportunity to escape.

Does Mikhail want me dead?

Did he hire a hit on me because I work for the FBI?

I stomp on the bald man's toes and slam my elbow into his groin.

He grunts and is momentarily stunned, releasing my arm from his grasp. "Get back here!" he shouts, doubled over in pain.

Right, like I'm going to wait for him to kill me. Did he think that I wouldn't fight back? He underestimates my desire for survival.

I race in the opposite direction of the vehicle, toward the main road, for help, screaming to get anyone else's attention.

Sergei chases after me. His footsteps grow louder and closer.

I glance over my shoulder and make the mistake of seeing him catching up with me. But that's not all I notice; the bald man has something in his hand.

I get only a glimpse. Is it a gun? He gives no warning that he's going to shoot me, and why would he if he wants me dead?

A jolt of electricity courses through my body.

The bastard has a stun gun.

I fall to the ground, unable to run or fight back.

Sergei scoops me into his arms and carries me back to the awaiting vehicle.

He could have killed me. Why didn't he?

———————

I awaken in a cold, dark cell. A single overhead bulb illuminates the room. The ground is chilly and hard. It's made of cement. The walls are brick and thick from the looks of it.

There are no windows. No evidence of the outside world from my vantage point.

There is a set of wooden stairs that leads upstairs. But to where? Am I back at Mikhail's home?

Is this his prison?

I'm caged in the cellar, my ankles bolted and chained. My hands aren't bound, but I have no tools to pick the lock or weapons to defend myself.

The room is small and dusty. It could have been used to hold wine a hundred years ago.

I'm its sole prisoner, confined to death.

Why lock me up if they are going to kill me? None of it is making any sense.

From above, there are heavy footsteps against the floorboards. Someone is pacing the length of the room.

There are muffled voices, loud and gruff. I can't understand what's being said or whose voices I hear. The conversation between the men becomes more intense. Shouts from two men battle back and forth. I sense it in one of the man's tones.

Desperation.

Is he pleading for his life?

My mouth goes dry, and my fingers tremble as I fiddle with the metal binds around my ankles. I have no tools, my purse isn't on me, my shitty phone is abandoned, and my shoes have been confiscated.

A gunshot rings out, and a loud thud follows as something or someone hits the floor.

Heavy footsteps tromp over the floor above. A minute later, someone is unlocking the cellar door.

Someone is coming down the stairs. It's dark and difficult to see the male figure, but it's not Mikhail, from the physique and height.

He steps under the single illuminating bulb, and my breath catches in my throat. Carlos Sanchez, the leader of the cartel. He's the last person I expect to see come down into the cellar.

"Carlos," I breathe, staring up at him.

"You know who I am, good." He beams. "My reputation travels far and wide. Unlike your boyfriend, who likes to rule the city. He's nothing outside of this town."

My boyfriend? Does he think Mikhail and I are together?

"Why kidnap me and bring me here?" I ask.

What happens when they realize I'm a federal agent and not the girlfriend of a bratva leader? I'm as good as dead.

Carlos bends down but keeps ample distance between us. "Why do you think? We want to hurt Mikhail."

I scoff at his suggestion. "Well, we broke up. Your intelligence is lacking."

I foolishly grabbed the wrong cell phone on my way to lunch. I'd been in such a rush to get away from Aaron that I hadn't realized I picked up the phone that I used while undercover. They must have used my decoy phone to track me and intercept the rideshare request.

"And dead," Carlos says. "Sergio can't go back to working with Mikhail. Now that you know he works for me, the jig is up."

"Sergio? Do you mean Sergei?"

Carlos chuckles and rises to his feet. "His real name was Sergio. He became Sergei to infiltrate the Russians."

"What are you planning to do?" I ask. I can't imagine he's going to just let me walk free, and Mikhail isn't going to give a damn what happens to me. We're not together. We never really were a couple.

"Don't you worry your pretty little head about that. I have more important matters for you to assist me with."

If it means getting out of the chains and the cellar, I'll take my chances.

I glance down, trying not to look intimidating or threatening. He doesn't know that I'm FBI, and I don't want him to be the least bit suspicious about me.

I let my voice quiver. It's not incredibly hard, given the circumstances. "What do you want me to do?" I ask.

"Call Mikhail. Tell him you want to see him."

That's it? I breathe a sigh of relief. They're underestimating me, which is good, but getting out of these chains will take more work than just making a phone call. "I don't have my phone."

"You can use mine," he says. Carlos shoves his hand into his pants pocket and retrieves his cell phone, handing me the device.

I don't know Mikhail's number, which would be strange for a girlfriend. But I can work with it. "I didn't memorize his number. It's saved into my phone."

He rolls his eyes, grabs the cell phone, and dials Mikhail, putting the call on speaker.

"Who is this? How did you get my number?" Mikhail answers his phone.

His voice sends warm, tingly feelings churning inside of me. "It's me," I say, as if he'd recognize my voice anywhere. "Your *Kisa*."

It's not like I know Mikhail that well, but he had called me *Kisa* multiple times. I can only hope that he'll realize that I'm in trouble, that I'd never refer to myself as that without being under duress.

Especially now, while he knows of my betrayal and hates me.

Mikhail clears his throat, and his voice is low and deeper. "Where are you, *Kisa*?" he asks. He sounds sexy, rough, and raspy. "I'd love to get you in my bed, finish what we started in the shower this morning."

We were never in the shower this morning. He's trying to give me a clue. Or maybe he's playing along because he knows that I'm in danger.

How do I tell him that Sergei is behind my abduction and the cartel is holding me against my will?

Carlos rips the phone from my grip and ends the call.

"What are you doing?" I gasp. Didn't he want to talk to Mikhail?

Carlos holds up a finger for me to wait. The cell phone in his hand rings, and he answers it.

"Now that I've gotten your attention, I want your men to back off on my merchandise."

"Which merchandise are we talking about?" Mikhail asks.

He doesn't bother to take the call off speakerphone. "I don't discuss specifics over the phone," Carlos says.

"Where and when?" Mikhail asks. "It should be someplace public and—"

"No," Carlos interrupts. "We do this my way if you want to see your girl alive. One hour, come to my complex. You know where that is, right?"

"Yes."

Carlos grins at me and ends the call. His two gold teeth glint under the dim bulb. "You're coming with me. I hear you're a nurse."

He retrieves a set of handcuffs from his back pocket. "First, you put these on. Then I'll take off the ankle restraints."

I hold out my arms, and he snaps the metal cuffs onto my wrists. I don't fight him, not yet, while I'm still secured to the floor.

Satisfied that he has me under his control, he unlocks the bindings around my ankles. "Come with me," he says and leads me up the rickety wooden staircase.

The air is musky and stale upstairs, just as bad as the cellar. Where the hell are we?

There's dust in every corner and sheets covering the furniture. This isn't where Carlos lives, and it's not his complex, where Mikhail is meeting him.

Bile rises to my throat, and I swallow it back down.

Carlos set Mikhail up. I don't know what's waiting for Mikhail at the complex, but I'm not there. There won't be any negotiations or chance he'll rescue me and take me home.

I doubt he'd set me free. He probably won't even show up to offer Carlos what he wants. Why would he? I'm just a girl who burned him from the inside out.

He hates me, and I don't blame him.

"Where are we?" I ask. My voice is soft and unthreatening. My hands are still bound, but they're in front of me, allowing me to fight back when the time is right.

Not yet. Not with Carlos and his men prowling the area. I don't want to experience another stun gun on my back or, worse, a bullet to the head.

Carlos escorts me through the kitchen and past Sergei's body. He's lying on the floor in a pool of his blood. He steps over the corpse like he's a child's toy that hasn't been picked up. "This way," he says, expecting me to follow.

There are two members of the cartel seated at the kitchen table with guns in their hands, watching me. It's like they're waiting to kill me, itching to pull the trigger.

I obediently follow Carlos through the kitchen, and then he leads me up a back stairwell to the second story. The house is filled with cobwebs. The place has been vacated for quite some time.

"I need you to fix him," Carlos says as he leads me into a bedroom. A man is lying on the mattress, his face red, and he's groaning.

"I can't do anything with my hands like this," I say, showing him the handcuffs.

Carlos grumbles and shoves the key into the lock, removing the cuffs.

"Do you have any medical supplies?" I ask as I approach the patient. His forehead is glistening with sweat. By the looks of it, I'd surmise he's running a fever.

"Not much," Carlos admits and glances around the room. "We haven't been here in a while."

"The dust gave it away," I say.

Carlos backhands me across the face. "Watch your tone. You're a prisoner, not a guest." The recent bruise that Aaron left on my skin throbs all over again. I wince and examine the patient. "I'm Madisyn," I say to the patient, introducing myself.

"Reece," he rasps. He's wincing in agony as he speaks.

Why is he trying to hide his discomfort?

"I'm a nurse. Can I ask you a few questions?"

He nods weakly. His cheeks are red, his pupils wide, but the room is dimly lit. I open the curtains and allow more light to filter into the room.

"Do you have any recent injuries or infections?" I ask as I approach his bedside to better look at him. His cheeks are flushed.

I don't know what I'm dealing with other than the cartel and a heap of trouble.

His eyes are glassy and he glances past me at Carlos.

"I may have sustained an injury," he says. He's careful how he answers. I suspect Carlos is behind that injury but mustn't want him dead like Sergei.

"May I see it?" I ask, keeping my tone calm and gentle.

He lifts his shirt, and there's an obvious sign of infection around what appears to be a recent stab wound. The wound is red and swollen.

"Your injury is infected," I say. "We need to get you antibiotics."

"There aren't any here. What other suggestions do you have?" Carlos says.

I shuffle away from the bed and stalk toward Carlos. "Aside from taking him to a hospital?"

At least the bratva were prepared when their associate had been injured. Mikhail had ensured that his men could have proper medical care at the medical center or in his home.

"That's out of the question."

"This place isn't the least bit sterile. You don't have the necessary medical equipment to tend to his injuries. He needs his wound cleaned and bandaged. He should have had stitches, but it's too late for that at this point."

"Can't you mash up ingredients and make a paste? Something to put on his wound to prevent the infection from getting worse and out of control."

"He needs antibiotics. His wound needs to be properly cared for, and this environment is not up to the standards that he requires. Take him to your complex."

"Excuse me? You don't give orders," Carlos says. He steps closer, his breath hitting me in the face.

"If you want your friend to get medical treatment, then at least take him somewhere that I can find the necessary ingredients to make a poultice. I need a clean compress, herbs, Epsom salt, and a variety of other ingredients that I'm not going to find in the kitchen downstairs."

His jaw snaps shut, and he grinds his teeth. "Fine." He grabs my arm and drags me back down the stairs.

I hide the evidence of pain, swallowing back the discomfort from his tight grasp as his fingers dig into my arm.

He drags me down the stairs to the main level. His men glance up as we hurry through the kitchen. Neither seems particularly busy. One man has a knife in his hand, and he's peeling an apple. The other is playing on his cell phone. From the looks of it, he's scrolling through one of those social media sites.

"Get him downstairs, pronto!" Carlos shouts at his men as he whisks me into the grimy living area.

He opens the front door and drags me outside.

My feet crunch over the cold, snowy ground. The bottoms of my feet ache from the ice as I take each step toward the awaiting vehicle.

I shiver. My clothes aren't warm enough for the weather, and I'm without a coat, shoes, or even a winter hat.

The black SUV is parked out front along with a two-door sedan. I get a better look at our surroundings. We're in the middle of nowhere, with trees surrounding us at every angle.

There are no other buildings or people nearby. They took me to a remote location. If they wanted me dead, they'd have killed me already.

He opens the back door of the vehicle. "Get in!"

While I don't want to do as he commands, my feet burn from the cold, and I oblige, climbing into the back seat.

Carlos slams the door behind me.

His men follow out the front door, with Reece grimacing in pain. Reece has one arm slung over each of the men as they drag him outside.

Briefly, they exchange words in Spanish, their voices low, making it difficult to hear the conversation from inside the SUV.

Carlos opens the back door, and they toss Reece in beside me.

"Keep him alive," Carlos says. He slams the back door, locking me in with the injured man.

Sweat glistens on Reece's forehead. His breathing is shallow and ragged. He shivers, and I can't tell if it's from the cold or the fever racing through him.

CHAPTER FOURTEEN

MIKHAIL

"ARE YOU SURE ABOUT THIS?" Luka asks.

He's the only man who knows what's going on with Madisyn. Sure, a few of them realize I brought her up to my room and showed her a good time, but they don't all know she's a federal agent and betrayed me.

The list of men who know of her betrayal is short. I can't have my men questioning my competence.

And Luka is the only one to know that she's been taken by the Sanchez Cartel.

He's driving the vehicle, and I'm riding in the passenger seat. We're en route to the cartel's compound. Is that where they're keeping Madisyn, or do they have her holed up some place else?

It's no secret the cartel has at least a dozen safe houses throughout the city. Probably more outside New York. They have an intricate network and sophisticated operation, but typically, kidnapping pretty girls doesn't fall under their repertoire.

"No, but I can't risk leaving her in Carlos Sanchez's hands," I say.

For a moment, I had considered contacting the FBI and offering myself up to save Madisyn.

It was a fleeting thought and one that was quickly squashed the moment my phone rang and I heard her voice.

She's alive.

The cartel would have already killed her if they intended to murder her and gloat about their accomplishments. They want something that happens to be a piece of my business.

It's not like I can't afford to give up a stake of my operation, specifically smuggling heroin, which I assume they're asking for but wouldn't say over the phone.

"Do you think showing up without an army is the right move?" Luka asks.

He's a good man and would die for me, like any good bratva soldier. I tried to let him marry my little sister, but she wanted nothing to do with him.

"I'm not afraid of Carlos or the cartel," I say.

We drive up to the iron-clad gates of the cartel's compound. We're going in through the front entrance.

Luka glances at me but hides any hint of nervousness or doubt.

His phone buzzes.

"We don't have time to deal with our men," I say. "Let it go to voicemail."

The cartel guard clicks the button in his booth, and ever so slowly, the gate begins to creep open. I exhale a heavy sigh.

After Luka's phone is silent, mine begins to ring. I glance at the caller ID. It's Dmitri.

Luka gently taps the gas pedal, and we head in through the open gates and along the wide driveway that leads up to the front door.

Carlos isn't outside, but a half dozen of his men, armed with guns, are waiting for us.

"Not now," I say as I answer the phone. "I'm dealing with something."

"Well, you have something to deal with even bigger at the house," Dmitri answers.

There's commotion in the background, a lot of it. I can hear the paper shredder at full speed eating pages of documents.

The pit of my stomach grows sour. "The FBI is here," Dmitri says.

He ends the call, giving me no indication of why they're barging into my home or what evidence they have for a warrant.

I can't deal with it now. Even if I wanted to, we're on the cartel's property, and they're swarming around the vehicle with guns drawn.

"Get out!" one of their men shouts as he stands outside the door.

Luka shuts off the vehicle, and we step out. The cartel guards are rough and thorough as they search us for weapons, disarming us, before shoving us inside through the front door.

There's no sign of Carlos or Madisyn.

Where is she?

"Where's Madisyn?" I shout at the armed guards, particularly those who dragged me from the vehicle and shoved me up the stairs and inside. His eyes are dark, lifeless.

The cartel is notorious for their shady dealings along with trafficking drugs and guns, but kidnapping isn't something I'm aware they've dealt in before. Are they moving up the ranks with trafficking people, not just goods, across the border?

"We get to ask the questions," Carlos says as he descends the staircase, sharply dressed, but there is a smidgen of blood on his cheek.

My mouth is dry, and I ball my hands into fists at my sides.

"Where is Madisyn?" I ask again. This time, the question is directed at the leader of the cartel, not his soldiers.

He straightens his tie and stalls in front of a mirror, admiring his reflection before answering my question.

"She's working for me."

His answer is baffling. I can't genuinely imagine that she wants to do his bidding. "Excuse me?"

What the hell is he talking about? Has he lost his mind, or does he have something on her? No, if that were the case, then the FBI would be combing through the cartel's place of business and home rather than mine.

Nausea sets in at the realization that my house is being trashed and torn apart by the Feds. What are they searching for? Is it because of Aaron Moore? Did he try to set me up? I wouldn't put it past the man. He terrorizes Madisyn, and the evidence on her face is enough to make me want to pummel the man and tear him to shreds.

Did the FBI realize that Madisyn hadn't returned from lunch? Had they suspected that I was behind her abduction?

"You heard me," Carlos says as he approaches. He gestures for his soldiers to step aside so that he can come and stand face-to-face with me. With his beady eyes, he glances me over, displeased with my appearance. Shaking his head, he strokes his jaw. "I don't know what that girl sees you in. She could do so much better."

"She is a ten," I say, wanting to convince him that she belongs to me. I don't want any of my secrets spilled to the cartel. And Carlos is a man who would force her, painfully so, to leak every detail that she's ever seen or heard, no matter how trivial. "Where is she?"

He steps closer and grins. "She's tending to one of my men."

I throw back my fist and land a blow to his face. The sound of bones crunching offers little relief. What are they making her do?

The guard who brought me inside the cartel's compound drags me off Carlos and slams his weapon against my head before cocking the safety off and pointing the barrel at my temple.

"Madisyn!" I shout, staring up at the staircase, assuming that she's being kept upstairs because that's where Carlos came from. But she could be anywhere.

He retrieves a handkerchief from his jacket and checks to see if blood drips from his nose. You can break a man's nose without causing blood to gush.

His nose is crooked, which seemingly matches his personality. I want to pound the shit out of him, but I don't think his men will let me continue. I'd likely be shot dead by the ass standing next to me with his gun at my head.

"She's preoccupied with another one of my men at the moment," Carlos says and chuckles at his remark. "Put that down." He gestures to his man defending him, and the gun by my temple is lowered.

"How'd you know she's mine?" Giving up anything to save Madisyn isn't wise for the organization and my men. But I'm here, against better judgment. And mainly, I have a sneaking suspicion that something more sinister is going on behind my back.

And this time, Madisyn isn't the culprit.

At least I don't think she is, and there'd be no reason for her to saddle up with the cartel to win her way back to me. It doesn't make sense.

Carlos chuckles under his breath and puts the handkerchief back in his coat. "Do you think that I'd give up all my secrets?"

"Maybe you don't have her at all," I say. "Your men have been running cons for years. The voice on the other end of the phone could have been simulated to sound like Madisyn."

The smile on the cartel leader's face disappears. "You want to see your girlfriend? Aaron!" Carlos shouts from the front entranceway.

Aaron?

It can't be the same Aaron who is Madisyn's ex-boyfriend and with the FBI, that's just too much of a coincidence. Aaron is a fairly common name; it must be someone else.

It doesn't matter how much I wish that it was a different Aaron, the same smug bastard who showed up at Madisyn's home the other night waltzes down the stairs, his hand on the banister, looking smug as shit.

I want to wipe that smile off his face and pound his head on the floor. The man deserves a thorough beating after the way he treated Madisyn. It's disgusting.

How much does Carlos know about Aaron?

"Better yet, you give me Madisyn, and I tell you about the undercover FBI agent you're working with," I say. "One of your men is a Fed."

Carlos glances over his shoulder at Aaron. "Do you mean this guy?" He jabs his thumb in Aaron's direction. "Aaron is one of my most loyal associates. I'm aware that he works for the FBI. How do you think we've managed to have them look the other way for so long?"

"Your loyal man over here likes to rough up women," I say. "Gave her that black eye that she's wearing."

"She's been fucking this guy," Aaron says, gesturing at me. "She deserves a reminder of who she belongs to."

Carlos isn't the least bit fazed by my remark or Aaron's. "What becomes of the girl doesn't matter much to me. I thought it would be fun to invite you over to see who she chooses."

"This is your idea of an invitation?" The cartel is crazier than I ever gave them credit for in the past.

"It's a compromise. I release the girl, and you give up your right to sell heroin. The cartel will be the exclusive seller. Unless you want to work for me and deal our product?"

I scoff at his suggestion. "I'm not working for you."

Carlos smirks, not the least bit surprised by my answer. "Do we have a deal?"

"No," I say. "Let Madisyn leave with me, and I won't burn your home to the ground."

"You don't have it in you," Carlos says and folds his arms across his chest.

He's goading me.

I bite my tongue to keep from revealing that I've done a plethora of terrible deeds, murdering men, threatening women and children. I'm no saint. I don't pretend to be a good guy because I'm not one.

Aaron is an FBI agent, and whether he is undercover or a dirty agent working with Carlos, I can't take the chance that anything I say will be recorded. I don't have the advantage of searching him for a wire or any other devices planted on him.

Carlos gives orders to one of his men to retrieve Madisyn. His associate heads upstairs and, several minutes later, returns with her. His fingers are tight around her arm.

There's dried blood caked to her fingers, and her hair is disheveled. Her feet are bare, and she winces as she's dragged forcefully down the stairs and shoved beside Carlos.

"It's a pleasure to see you again," Carlos says with a wry grin, staring at Madisyn. He glances her up and down, leering at her breasts.

"That's enough!" I snarl at Carlos, and my fist slams across his jaw. Unfortunately, I don't seem to break or so much as dislocate it.

What a shame.

I'd have liked to have scored twice against his ass and taught the filthy vermin a lesson.

One of his guards drags me off his ass, pushing me backward several feet to keep an adequate distance between me and their boss.

Madisyn's eyes grow wide as she glances from me to Aaron. I'm not sure who she despises more.

"What's going on?" Madisyn asks.

Carlos beams with pride. I don't have the slightest clue what's running through that man's head. But I have a feeling whatever he's got planned isn't going to make my life any easier. "They're going to fight for you."

"Fight for me?" Her brow is furrowed, and she glances at Aaron, and then her gaze lands on me. She takes a tentative step backward.

Where does she think she's going to go?

How far will she get? There's no chance the cartel is going to let her walk out.

She stumbles backward several feet before one of the guards catches her. His fingers dig into her bare arms, leaving a lasting impression against her skin. "Don't move," he whispers a little too loudly, for just about everyone in the vicinity to overhear.

Madisyn struggles against his grip before relenting.

"Let her go," I say. "Your quarrel is with me. Madisyn has nothing to do with this negotiation." It's not much of a negotiation considering that she's been held against her will, as far as I can determine.

Carlos strokes his chin before dropping his hands to his sides. "Come with me." He takes off down the hallway, and when I don't move quickly enough to follow him, one of his men jabs me in the back with his gun.

———

"You're not seriously going to go through with this over some girl?" Luka is at my side.

Is he trying to convince me to give her up to Aaron?

No way in hell am I letting that asshole lay a finger on Madisyn.

She's mine.

And while I'm still pissed at her and want nothing to do with her, somehow, I've managed to get myself involved in a 'fight night' with the cartel. We're escorted down into the basement and through a corridor of dark tunnels until we reach a small room to get ready.

It feels like we've been walking for miles.

"Strip down. There are shorts in the bin," one of the men says as he points at a bin by the wall.

The room is tiny. There are no windows and no other exits, only the door we came through. There's no escaping the room.

I throw a jab at the guard's face, and his neck whips back. Within seconds, he's got his gun poised on me. "Don't make me piss off the boss," he says, pushing the barrel into my forehead.

"Go ahead, shoot me."

His gaze tightens. "No, I'll shoot the pretty girl, your prize, first. And make you watch."

Luka subtly shakes his head, warning me that this man isn't worth the hassle.

The guard slams the door shut behind us and latches it shut. We're locked inside. Wonderful. How the hell am I getting out of this mess?

"Any news at home?" I ask, glancing at Luka.

He reaches for his phone. The cartel is sloppy. They checked us for weapons but didn't so much as steal our phones. I was careless, leaving mine in the vehicle outside.

"No signal," Luka says. He carries his phone around the small room, lifting it higher as if that will help him get a signal to make a call. Who is he going to call?

Are the Feds really at the compound? If they are, maybe I am safer here with the cartel.

"This is ridiculous," Luka says and shoves his phone back into his pocket. "You can't fight that guy out there. You'll kill him."

"That's the point."

I'm not the least bit bashful as I strip out of my clothes and reach for a pair of black gym shorts in the bin. I lift them to my nose and grimace at the stench. They haven't been cleaned and reek of sweat and blood.

I opt to wear my black boxers that were underneath my clothes. They'll suffice for Aaron's ass-kicking.

"The cartel is setting you up, sir. Carlos will blame you for killing Aaron, a federal agent, and will have you arrested."

"He's not stupid enough to bring the Feds into his home," I say.

The lights flicker, and the roar of the crowd ripples through the small room. It's practically a closet, but the walls are made of brick and aren't budging.

Heavy footfalls approach the door, and the clasp of the lock clicks as one of the cartel's men pulls open the door. "It's time."

"Sir, let me fight in your place," Luka says.

It's noble, but I'm not letting him get in the ring with Aaron. I want to punch the son of a bitch who left a mark on Madisyn's face. Aaron had no right to touch her.

"That's not going to happen," I say. "This is my fight."

"Come with us," the guard says and gestures for us to step out into the hallway and follow him.

He's not alone. A second guard accompanies him, and both have their guns ready if we try to fight. While the thought has briefly crossed my mind, I don't know where they're keeping Madisyn, and I didn't show up to abandon the mission and leave her behind.

She's coming with me and going to pay for her betrayal.

We follow down the long, narrow hallway. It's dimly lit and grungy. The basement could use a scrub and a fresh coat of paint. The sound carries men's boisterous shouts and cheers as we grow near.

There's a cage in the center of the room. Overhead halogen bulbs brighten the dark, damp space.

Already, there are dozens of men lined up, drinking and cheering on the activities to come. Men are taking bets, specifically Carlos's men.

Aaron stalks in from the opposite end of the room. Another hallway leads into the pit.

"You've got this," Luka says, cheering me on.

I don't need his reassurances. "Find Madisyn," I say, leaning closer into his ear. "Get her out of here."

The lights overhead flicker once again. Carlos steps into the crowd and the jeers and excitement further intensify. It's as if electricity flows straight into the heart of the cage as the men step aside for the cartel leader.

They're making way for us to fight.

Carlos opens the metal cage door and gestures to step in first. I don't suppose that he will lock me into the enclosure and leave me. There'd be quite a lot of disappointed attendees.

He begins the announcement, introducing me as if I need any introduction. The booing commences, and when I win the fight, I'm beginning to question how I will get out of here.

Is Carlos a man of his word?

One problem at a time.

The crowd parts ways for Aaron as they cheer him on as he steps into the cage to fight. He's wearing a bright red shiny satin robe.

It seems fitting since I'm the bull that will decimate his ass.

"There can only be one winner. The man who comes out alive," Carlos says and chuckles. He's enjoying this a little too much.

He doesn't know that I've fought men twice my size, murdered and slaughtered criminals who betray me. I don't need a weapon to take his life. I have my bare hands.

Aaron drops his robe at the edge of the cage against the metal wire.

"Five!"

The countdown begins.

I'm quick on my feet, and Aaron throws a punch in my direction before Carlos reaches 'one.' No one seems to care that he's a cheat.

But I anticipate it because I'd do the same if I thought I was going to get my ass kicked.

Lucky for me, I have the advantage. While he's taller by a few inches, I'm more muscular. I've fought dozens of men. While he was Pakhan, my father threw me into the ring to learn to defend myself.

I dodge his shot and catch a glimpse of metallic shining under the light in his hand.

Aaron has a blade in his palm.

"Didn't think you had a chance without a knife?" I mock him.

The chaotic noise of the crowd surrounds us and jeers at me, cheering his lame-ass on.

Aaron's gaze flinches at my remark.

Oh, he heard me.

A spectator launches a beer bottle at the cage. It crashes against the metal wire but startles me long enough for Aaron to scratch me with the tip of his knife.

The wound is superficial. I'll survive. I've suffered worse at the hands of men who had a reason to want me dead.

What's his reason?

Is it because I slept with Madisyn, and he's a jealous ass?

"I want you dead," Aaron says, and his top lip snarls as he stares at me with disgust. "You're never going to lay another finger on my girlfriend."

"Your girlfriend?" I've had enough of dancing around with him in the ring. It's time to knock his ass out. "Madisyn isn't your girlfriend. She doesn't want anything to do with you." I throw a mean right hook that's bound to leave a mark tomorrow.

He doesn't go down, but I didn't expect him to go after one punch. He's probably taken a beating or two when he trained at Quantico.

He likely knows how to fight like a federal agent, not a Russian.

He *will* go down. I'll make sure of it.

Through the noise and the surrounding chaos, I catch a glimpse of the bright red robe that Aaron wore moments earlier.

Madisyn has it wrapped around her body. She's swimming in the satin material.

She's cheering for him.

CHAPTER FIFTEEN

MADISYN

CARLOS'S MEN parade me around like I'm a trophy.

Felix, one of Carlos' associates, forced me to undress and change into a black lace bra and underwear set that leaves nothing to the imagination.

I'm exposed and on display. My clothes are stolen from me before I'm shucked out of the closet and dragged into the spotlight.

"Our prize for the evening," Carlos announces as I enter the chaotic scene.

The men are boisterous, several of them tossing empty beer bottles at the cage in the middle of the basement.

Thankfully, they don't pay me very much attention, their focus on the two men throwing jabs back and forth in the cage.

Aaron and Mikhail are going at it.

I can't imagine it's a fair fight. Aaron is a highly-trained FBI agent, but he hasn't had a lot of street fighting experience. Then again, I also didn't suspect that he was running with the cartel.

I betrayed Mikhail.

Aaron betrayed me. Not that we're together. I don't want anything to do with him.

I wrap my arms around myself, but it's chilly.

Felix pushes me closer to the cage. "Enjoy the entertainment," he whispers into my ear. He's giving me a front-row seat, but I don't want it.

Yet, I can't seem to look away, either.

"Stay here," Felix orders. He leaves me by the cage, heading toward Carlos to exchange a few words.

I can't tell what's being said, but they're both momentarily preoccupied.

There's a satin robe lying at the edge of the cage. I reach my small hand in, pull the red cloth through the metal bars, and wrap it around myself, pulling the sash around my waist.

I swim in the gown, but at least it covers me. How long until they force me out of the red material and put me on display once again?

Mikhail breaks his concentration with Aaron, locking eyes on me. It's only for an instant, and he pays the price.

Aaron has a switchblade in his grasp and tears at Mikhail's flesh. He's lucky it's not impaled.

The crowd cheers for Aaron, but Mikhail hasn't slowed or faltered. Both men ignore me as they throw punch after punch, landing blow upon blow on each other's bodies.

It's painful to watch.

Aaron doesn't play clean or fair. He slams on Mikhail's bare feet and trips him, knocking him to the ground.

"Is that how you want to play?" Mikhail shouts at his opponent.

Spit flies in the air between them as they pound the shit out of one another.

Aaron mutters something, but his back is to me. I can't make out the exchange between the two men.

Mikhail rips the blade from Aaron's grasp. It flies across the cage and hits the metal bars before clanking to the ground. "How about we fight like men?"

"You're not a man," Aaron shouts.

I pull the robe tighter, folding my arms across my chest. The air is chilly and stale. The room smells musty and of sweat. I don't want to watch, but I can't look away.

If Mikhail wins, what happens to me?

He isn't going to just let me go.

If Aaron wins, I'm not any better off. He'll treat me like a rag doll, toss me around. Abuse me. It's what he does. He treats me like garbage because it makes him feel better about himself.

I'm not waiting around to find out who wins and gets to claim me as their prize. I shuffle through the crowd, moving farther from the cage, when I stumble into one of Mikhail's men, Luka.

"Come with me," he whispers, latching onto my arm.

"Get off me! I'm not going anywhere with you." I yank myself free from his grasp. We catch Felix's attention when he realizes that I'm not standing by the cage where he left me to watch the fight.

"Suit yourself, but I'm not sticking around to see what happens," Luka says. He jets out through the rowdy crowd, managing to disappear.

I hurry after him. If he has a way out, I'm taking it.

"You're leaving your boss behind?" I trail behind him.

"You sound surprised," Luka says and smirks.

"I thought you bratva type all stick together."

He grabs my arm and leads me down a dark hallway. He yanks the first door on the right open and pushes me inside. He's right behind me. "Keep walking."

"You know your way around the cartel's home?" I ask.

"No. While Mikhail was fighting with your boyfriend, I was doing my own bit of reconnaissance."

"Aaron isn't my boyfriend." At least not anymore. He hasn't been for quite some time, and the thought of him touching me brings bile rising to my throat.

"Whatever." Luka doesn't seem to care either way. "My orders are to get you to safety."

"Your orders? Who do you work for?" I can't help but doubt his loyalty to Mikhail and the Russian Bratva. Sergei pretended to be loyal to Mikhail. How do I know that Luka isn't another sleeper agent?

"Mikhail Barinov," Luka says. He brushes past me and grabs my hand, dragging me through the tunnel. "Keep your voice down," he whispers.

I'm silent except for the breaths I take, as I'm both chilly and exhausted. Adrenaline pumps through my veins as we run through the dark path. There are a handful of doors every few hundred feet, and I can't even begin to fathom where they lead or if we're heading deeper into danger.

"This way," Luka says as he pulls open one of the doors, and we hurry through another corridor. "Slow down, try to look inconspicuous," he says.

How will I manage to do that wearing a bright red robe?

Footsteps clomp against the floor as a guard heads in our direction.

Luka shoves me up against the cold stone wall, his hands on my hips, his mouth pressed against mine.

The guard whistles approvingly as he breezes right past us.

Luka's fingers hike up my robe, and my eyes flash open.

What the hell is he doing? He's gone too far.

I knee him in the groin and slam my fist into his face.

He doubles over in agony.

Good!

"Sorry," Luka mutters. He's quick to apologize, but it's too late.

I stalk past him, heading in the direction where the guard had just come from. How come he didn't seem surprised to see us? Is this how the patrons had arrived to watch the fight?

He chases after me. "I'm sorry. I was trying to look convincing," he says.

I ignore his pleas as I push open the door at the end of the hallway. Freedom at last!

The door leads outside. The air is icy and cold. My breath hovers with each exhale that spills past my lips. There are dozens of unattended vehicles parked in an abandoned lot.

I don't quite recognize where we are other than still inside the city.

"We need to find a phone." It's too bad there aren't any payphones anymore. My cell phone is long gone. I tug the robe tighter. My feet are freezing on the cold asphalt.

Luka pulls out his cell phone and hands me the device. "Do you mean this?"

I want to kill him. "You've had that all along?"

"It didn't work inside the cartel's compound," Luka says. He unlocks his device. "We have a signal now, though."

"Give me that!" I snatch the phone from his grasp and dial Agent Kingston's cell phone.

"Agent Kingston," Barrett answers his phone.

I breathe a sigh of relief that he answers the call. It would have come up as an unfamiliar number. "Agent Kingston, it's Madisyn Taylor," I say, giving my undercover last name. If Luka and Mikhail's men haven't figured out my surname, Carter, I don't intend to give it to them.

"Where are you? We're at the Barinov residence and have torn apart this place searching for you."

"The cartel picked me up this afternoon. One of Carlos' men must have intercepted my rideshare request. I managed to escape with one of Mikhail's men, but you should know, sir, Aaron Moore is working with the cartel."

"Are you sure?"

"He's working with Carlos, and he's in an illegal fight with Mikhail right now. They're fighting for me as their prize. Luka and I managed to sneak out, but someone is bound to notice that we left. It won't be long until they're searching for both of us."

"I'll come to pick you up. Where are you?" he asks again.

I'm not sure of the exact location. "I'll drop a pin," I say, giving him the GPS information for him to send a team to help before I end the call.

I hand Luka his phone. "You should get out of here."

————

Agent Kingston arrives along with a SWAT unit. I'm whisked into the front seat of his vehicle, the heat on high blast.

The door, however, remains open, which doesn't help warm my feet, but I'm not as frigid as earlier.

I draw them a map, and the SWAT unit prepares to break into the facility.

"Any chance you have another pair of boots in the trunk?" I ask. I want to be part of the team that infiltrates the cartel and ends the fight.

"Shoes? You can't go tactical wearing that," Barrett says.

At least I'm still wearing the robe. It's not the least bit discreet. The flaming red stands out even in the dark, but it's better than striding around in my underwear.

He pops the trunk and retrieves his standard-issue FBI jacket, and drapes it over my shoulders. "You're staying here. Warm up, try to relax. You did good out there."

I don't feel the least bit good. Mikhail is still in the ring, fighting with Aaron. Assuming one of them hasn't killed the other one yet.

Every second feels like an hour passes as SWAT tears in through the same entrance where we made our escape.

Luka didn't heed my advice. He ran back into the chaos, trying to help Mikhail before the FBI arrived. He's loyal to a fault. Luka had the opportunity to save himself, but instead, he got me out and then went back for his boss.

The raid happens over a matter of minutes, but it goes by in slow motion. Men reappear from the darkened entrance wearing handcuffs, escorted out one at a time by the authorities.

I breathe a sigh of relief when Aaron is arrested. His face is red, his lip bloody, and his eye swollen.

"What are you doing? Get me out of these cuffs!" Aaron argues with one of the SWAT members.

I don't budge from my position at the edge of the vehicle, the warm air hitting my back, warming me while the cold caresses my cheeks.

"Madisyn, tell them I'm with the FBI and I don't belong in handcuffs."

I'm not telling them anything. The bastard deserves to see the inside of a cell.

"I'm with the FBI," Aaron pleads. "There's been a mistake. Barrett!" He locks eyes on my supervisor. My ex wreaks of desperation.

SWAT and several FBI agents continue to trail out of the basement with men in handcuffs. I've yet to see Mikhail.

There are a number of the cartel's men, including Felix, but there is no sign of Carlos.

Did he get out before the Feds began to raid the place? He could be hiding anywhere inside the compound. There were several tunnels and rooms in the basement, not including the main floor of the compound and the upstairs.

What about Mikhail and Luka?

More men, several unfamiliar faces, are brought out in handcuffs. They were spectators who gathered to watch the fight.

I shiver. The air is frosty when I recognize Mikhail being escorted out by one of the SWAT leaders. Luka is right behind him in handcuffs.

Mikhail is wearing nothing more than his underwear. His chest is red and will probably be bruised tomorrow. His cheek has a nice mark, and there's a visible cut, dripping with blood from the knife wound on his chest.

Unlike the others being led to the back of a squad car, he's being escorted to an ambulance.

I climb out of the vehicle and slide my arms into the FBI jacket as I hurry barefoot through the parking lot toward the commotion.

"Agent Carter." Barrett's tone is warning me to get back into the vehicle.

Well, I can't do that. My feet burn from the cold asphalt, but I hurry to the back of the ambulance, where they're putting Mikhail onto a stretcher.

"You made it out alive," I say.

"So did you," he whispers.

The EMTs lift him into the ambulance. Mikhail is in handcuffs, restrained. His gaze meets mine. He's holding back any hint of pain, but blood drips from the wound on his chest. The earlier one was superficial, but the second wound was worse.

His skin is glistening and pale. The EMT hooks up an I.V. to him and applies pressure to the wound, bandaging it up.

The anger that I expect isn't there. It's more like relief that floods through me.

"This isn't over, *Kisa*."

"I suppose it's not, but you're going to prison." I smile and take a step back, letting the EMTs deal with Mikhail while I head back to the vehicle. There isn't more for me to say. He was only supposed to be an assignment.

I wasn't supposed to sleep with Mikhail, the head of the bratva. And falling in love with him is out of the question.

But as I walk farther from the ambulance, I glance over my shoulder.

He quirks a grin because somehow he knows that he's gotten under my skin, and I won't be able to forget about him. Ever.

CHAPTER SIXTEEN

MIKHAIL

NINE WEEKS LATER...

The FBI has nothing on me. The search warrant for the bratva compound was strictly to find Madisyn.

They had to release me. Luka too.

"I want you to swing by Federal Plaza," I say to Luka.

"Do you think that's wise, sir?" Luka is behind the wheel.

Dmitri has been holding down the fort while I've been in and out of the hospital for surgery. If it's not one thing, it's another. The stab wound was deep and required stitches, but the fight ended up rupturing my spleen.

But I've come to trust Luka even more over the past few weeks. His loyalty to saving Madisyn will be repaid one day.

"No, but I want to see her."

Correction. I need to see her. It's been nine weeks since I've had my fix of Madisyn Taylor. At least that's the name that she gave me when she broke down.

Her real name is Madisyn Carter. I've managed to dig into her past.

Once a week, I cruise past her apartment in the city. Late at night, when she leaves the window shade open, I can see her in her bedroom, the lights on.

It's like she leaves her blinds open for me. Does she ever see me watching from my car out on the street, parked in front of her building?

I haven't approached her. I've kept my distance because I want to protect her.

Until the cartel members are prosecuted and their organization breaks apart, she will be a target, especially if they believe that we're together.

It's no wonder that her dimwitted ex-boyfriend didn't know it was all a ruse, our relationship. Well, it wasn't fake to me when it started, but that's a secret I'll be taking to my grave.

I fucked up and fell in love.

I can't let that happen again. I swear I won't, but there have been too many sleepless nights. I will get her back into my bed.

"There are other ways that are far more subtle," Luka says.

"You mean like running into her?" I'm not a subtle man. I work with a purpose, and if I want something, I take it.

"You could start with sending flowers."

"I don't send flowers." He can't be serious. I'm not the least bit soft or gentle. That's not how I operate.

Luka is desperately trying not to smile. "Right. You could send her a Glock."

"Very funny," I mutter under my breath. "I think giving a federal agent an illegal weapon isn't my best move."

He shrugs nonchalantly, his focus on the road. "It would get you in handcuffs, and she could frisk you."

He's a dead man.

"I'm done talking with you about Madisyn. How's your love life?" I'm bitter, and I don't even give a shit.

"About as non-existent as yours," Luka says. "We could go to the club, find a hot piece of ass? I'm sure there's some girl there who can satisfy your urges."

The idea makes me sick to my stomach. I don't want anyone else. I want Madisyn.

"No." I cut off his suggestion, not wanting to hear another word or thought about what he wants to do to some girl half his age. He likes chasing ass, and I'm only interested in chasing after Madisyn.

Damn, she's gotten to me.

Fuck.

"Okay. We could order you an escort?" Luka says.

That's his nice way of suggesting bringing a prostitute into the compound. I don't need to pay for sex. I can have any number of hot ladies I want. The problem is that those ladies aren't Madisyn. It doesn't matter how much they look like her or sound like her. They're not her.

I'm appalled at his remark. "Or we could kidnap Madisyn, and I can have my way with her."

Luka glances at me. "That is an option, but may I remind you what happened the last time she went missing? The Feds raided our compound, and we didn't even have her in our possession."

He's right.

But I don't care. I want her, and I want to have my way with her.

"Retrieve her and bring her to my home."

Luka's knuckles whiten as he grips the steering wheel. "And if she doesn't go willingly, sir?"

"She will." No doubt she's been in agony without my touch against her supple skin. She'll bend to my will, and I will break her if necessary.

———

I ensure my men have the compound in order, clean and, more importantly, anything incriminating locked up and hidden away.

Bringing her home is a risk, but one that I'm willing to take.

If I was an honorable man, I'd leave her alone, let her live her life, and forget about the moment that we shared.

But I'm not the least bit good. I pride myself on being brutal and ruthless. It's how I survived when my father was Pakhan and I was nothing more than a lowly prince.

With brutality comes strength. He taught me all that I know, and it is with his wisdom and guidance, I was able to take over the throne when he died.

It didn't come without a fight.

His men may have questioned my command, but never my loyalty. Now they fall at my feet if I demand it from them.

Except for Sergei.

He is the one mistake that keeps me up at night.

Well, aside from Madisyn. That woman is a vixen and had me deceived.

Sergei is lucky he's dead. If he weren't, I'd have gutted the bastard for what he did to the family.

I glance at my watch and grab my coat. "Let's go!" I shout at Luka.

"I thought you were waiting here?" Luka grabs the keys and accompanies me out to the SUV. He unlocks the doors and climbs into the driver's side to chauffeur me around.

I could drive, but he's also my bodyguard, and I appreciate the extra set of eyes around to make sure that we're not being followed. He's trained to anticipate the unexpected. I know my weaknesses and align myself with men who can keep me from ending up dead.

"I want to see Madisyn's face when we show up."

"Fair enough, boss."

I sit up front with Luka. We pull away from the compound and head across town in the opposite direction of her apartment. At least her rental had been closer, but I'm sure that was intentional while she was working undercover.

There's plenty of traffic, but we left with enough time to ensure that she hasn't gotten home from work yet.

Luka has been watching her activity, tailing her daily. She takes the subway, which means she'll be walking home instead of driving. It gives us time to pull up alongside her before she heads into her building.

We turn the corner, passing the subway station, and I catch sight of her bright red coat first, with her long vanilla locks halfway down her back.

The girl should be wearing a hat and scarf.

He slows the SUV to a crawl as we come up alongside Madisyn. I press the silver button, and the window rolls down.

She's shivering from the chill in the air. One glance in my direction, and her gloved hands are balled into fists. Madisyn exhales a heavy sigh, and her breath hangs in the air. "What do you want, Mikhail?"

The way she says my name makes my cock stir in my trousers. I shouldn't be this hellbent on one girl, but she's got me tied up inside, and I need to unravel the knot.

"Get in," I say, my tone firm and not the least bit friendly.

She glances from me to her building.

Is she trying to decide if she can run and make it inside before I catch her?

She stops walking, and Luka hits the brakes. The chilly air seeps into the vehicle, and I'm grateful when Luka blasts the heat.

Madisyn doesn't step any closer. "What do you want?" she asks and folds her arms across her chest. Her black leather gloves stand out amongst her bright red wool coat.

"I want you to get into the vehicle."

She glances around outside. It's growing dark, and there aren't any other pedestrians on the street.

Is she looking for someone to help?

After a moment, she shuffles near the SUV and pulls open the back door.

"That was easier than I thought," I mutter as she slams the door shut.

I shut the window. The heat begins to fill the void, warming the SUV once again. I shift around in my seat to face her.

Luka pulls the vehicle away from the curb and heads back to the compound.

"How are you?" I ask. I've wondered how she's been after what happened with the cartel. I'm grateful to Luka for getting her out before the raid. However, she is responsible for bringing in the Feds during the fight.

It was probably for the best, keeping me from having to kill a federal agent, well, an ex-agent at this point. He's in prison awaiting trial. It's been all over the news these past few weeks.

She laughs under her breath. "You didn't ask me to come to sit in the back seat so that you can see how I'm doing."

Madisyn is smart. I never gave her enough credit before.

"How's Aaron?" I ask with a wry grin.

"I haven't spoken with him, but he's behind bars. Just like you should be."

"Ouch." I pretend to be hurt by her remark. "You don't want to see me arrested." I'd like to think that I've managed to lull my way past her cool exterior. It's a front, a show that she has to put on because of her job.

Her gaze tightens, and she tilts her head slightly. "You do seem to have the uncanny ability to avoid prosecution."

"That's because there's no evidence."

She exhales a soft breath and secures her seatbelt. "Where are you taking me? If you intend on killing me, I'd prefer to at least have the opportunity to let my dog out and leave him with a neighbor."

"She doesn't have a dog," Luka says.

"I could have a dog," Madisyn quips. She leans forward. "You've been spying on me?"

"He's been making sure that you're safe and the cartel leaves you alone, on my orders." I don't want her jumping down Luka's throat. He doesn't deserve her wrath. If she wants to be angry with anyone, she can take her frustration out on me.

"I have my badge and a gun. I am an FBI agent, in case you've forgotten," Madisyn says.

My jaw clenches, and I grit my teeth. "I haven't forgotten." She has the uncanny ability to get under my skin. I want to teach her a lesson and make her beg for my forgiveness for what she did, her betrayal.

I exhale a long, slow breath. "Why did you get into the vehicle if you think we're going to kill you?"

She scoots back in the seat, making herself comfortable. Her shoulders relax, and she presses her lips together. But she doesn't answer.

Does Madisyn believe that I'm going to hurt her?

Yes, I'm capable of doing atrocious acts. I've threatened families and children, but only because I protected my own family.

Family who disowned me.

The bratva is my blood. The only family left who mean anything to me. My sister and her two children are gone, out of my life. She's playing house with one of my most hated enemies and raises the twins with him.

He is their father, but she should have been smarter and more careful.

But I never hurt her. Well, not without just cause. I may have let my anger take hold, but I let her go, freed her to be with the man she loves.

I still hate the bastard. I'm not too keen on her, either.

Family is the bonds we make, not the blood that runs through our veins. My brothers are the bratva, the men who are loyal, who would shed their blood to protect one another. They're devoted and honorable, men worth fighting for and at their side.

Madisyn doesn't answer my question about why she climbed into the SUV if she thought I would kill her. It's because she doesn't believe I intend to hurt her.

If I'd wanted her dead, she'd have already been buried and the evidence destroyed.

"How long is this going to take? I have a hot date tonight," Madisyn says.

I growl at her words. The thought of anyone else coming anywhere closer to her sets me on edge. "Give me your phone."

Her brow furrows, but she hands me her cell phone. "I guess you're going to want to frisk me, too."

A wry smile forms at the corners of my lips. Just imagining my fingers moving over every curve of her delicious ass makes my cock throb.

"I don't just want to. I have to frisk you," I say. The thought of pushing her up against a wall and spreading her legs makes me want to roll down the window.

Is it warm in here?

The last thing in the world I want is for Madisyn to realize that she has me under her thumb. No, I'm the one in control. Not her. That's how it has to be.

CHAPTER SEVENTEEN

MADISYN

WHY THE HELL did I go against better judgment and climb into the back seat of the bratva's vehicle?

Have I gone mad?

If Mikhail wanted me dead, he wouldn't have insisted on his associate getting me out of the cartel's compound several weeks ago.

He probably just wants to talk. And he's not the only one who needs to talk.

Although why couldn't he have done that here? By my apartment. Why drive to his home? At least that's the direction that his driver is heading.

"How long is this going to take?" I ask. I need to know what game Mikhail is playing. I owe him for getting me away from the cartel, and even more so, I owe him an apology for sleeping with him.

I'm not the kind of girl to mix work and pleasure. Except that is exactly what I did, and I can't stop thinking about his fingers digging into my hip, my body wrapped around his cock.

Mikhail glances me over. He can't see much with the wool coat and my black slip-on clogs.

Does he know that I'm suspended from work? Sleeping with the leader of the bratva is bad. I wouldn't have lost my job if I had come clean, but lying about it is problematic. At least according to the FBI's playbook.

I'm a rule-breaker, and as such, it means a thirty-day suspension with no pay.

I'm lucky that I'm not completely out of a job.

"Who are you meeting?" Mikhail asks, ignoring my question.

"What?"

Luka pulls the vehicle up to the front gates of the bratva compound. My stomach does donuts like on an icy road, spinning wildly out of control.

"You mentioned that you have a hot date tonight. Who is it with?" Mikhail is back on me with his interrogation.

"It's no one you know," I lie. I don't have a date. I just wanted to see if he'd be jealous. He seems like the jealous type, like he wouldn't be willing to share me with another man.

It's probably for the best. I don't think I could handle two possessive men at once.

I quirk a grin as Luka puts the engine in park and the doors unlock. I checked the child safety latch when I got into the vehicle. I open the door and step out, stretching my legs.

He practically leaps out of the vehicle to finish his interrogation. He's as bad as the FBI when it comes to demanding an answer on the spot. "Who is it?" Mikhail growls at me.

"Why do you want to know? Are you jealous?"

He pins me with his stare. "You're mine for tonight. Whoever you're meeting, tell them you're not going to make it."

He shoves my phone back into my grasp.

I open my mouth, surprised that he isn't keeping my phone. He also hasn't searched me yet for a weapon.

I open my text messages and glance at them briefly before shoving my phone back into my pocket. There were no new messages, not that I was expecting anything.

There is no hot date.

Unless you count a carton of ice cream and a romance movie in front of the television. Not that Mikhail needs to know what I had planned. It's none of his business.

"Come inside," Mikhail says. It's not an invitation. It's an order. He grabs my hand and leads me in through the front door.

My breath catches in my throat, and I obediently obey and follow him inside. Luka is a few feet behind us and shuts the door after stepping inside.

Mikhail whisks me down the hall into the study and closes the pocket door behind us.

"What are we doing?" I ask, not understanding why he brought me to his home.

"Have a seat." He gestures to the sofa.

"I'd rather stand." I fold my arms across my chest, my coat still secure although I'm getting warm.

"Okay, stand. Are we going to talk about what you did?"

"What I did?" I scoff at his question.

"You slept with me. Was that all part of your little assignment?" Mikhail asks. He steps closer, closing the distance between us.

I don't move. My body has frozen in place.

Mikhail reaches out, brushing a strand of hair behind my ear.

I flinch and a shiver ripples through me. Does he notice the effect that he has on me? I clear my throat, trying to hide the heat building within me.

"Was it?" He's less patient than I remember. Even when he's angry with me, there's a warmth and a passion that he exudes.

My voice is soft, and my question is barely above a whisper. "Do you hate me?" I need to know the truth because if the roles were reversed, I'm not sure that I'd have it within me to forgive him. I've been burned one too many times.

"I should," Mikhail says. "I ought to hate you, vow never to speak to you again."

My lips part, and I exhale an even, slow breath. "I deserve that," I say. My gaze falls to the floor. Why did he bring me here? To taunt me and tease me? Does he want to remind me how I hurt him and how much he hates me?

"Well, it isn't what I want." Mikhail is back on me. This time, his fingers are in my hair. He grabs a fistful of my blonde locks, tugging on the tresses, guiding my face up to his. "I want you, *Kisa.*"

Each breath I take grows louder, deeper, raspier. I want him too. But he's bratva. He's everything I can't be. I'm good. He's evil.

But the world isn't quite so black and white.

He saved my life.

Well, technically, his comrade rescued my ass, but it was on Mikhail's orders. He was trying to stay alive while I escaped.

"It's against the rules," I say, staring up into his darkened, heated gaze.

His voice doesn't falter. He's louder and more forceful with his question. "Whose rules?"

My mouth is dry. I'm already in trouble with my job. If I'm associating with Mikhail, I'll never have another opportunity with the bureau. "It's against the rules to associate with a known felon."

"I haven't been convicted," Mikhail boasts.

He's not wrong, but the semantics don't matter. The Office of Professional Responsibility is already up my ass for lying to them, sleeping with him, and having any sort of relationship at all will ensure that I lose my job.

His lips close in on mine, and I gasp from the pressure building and the blazing inferno inside of me. Mikhail pulls me tighter against his body, and I can feel his excitement growing between us.

"I want you, *Kisa*."

"You could have anyone," I say.

Why does he want me?

I'm a nobody, a girl who betrayed him. Is he doing this to get back at me? To show me what it feels like to be the fool?

He captures my lips again, but this time, there's a roughness that he exudes. He's pushing my jacket over my shoulders, and the wool coat thuds softly to the floor.

My current thoughts are pushed far from my head as his fingers guide my neck to the side. He kisses a path across my neck, claiming me.

I yelp as he leaves his mark on my skin, biting my collarbone. My neck is exposed as he drags his tongue over my flesh and his fingers inch my skirt higher.

His touch sets my body on fire.

Mikhail backs me up against the window. The cool glass pane sends a shiver through me.

"Cold?" he whispers, nipping at my neck.

"Yes," I whisper, answering him with the truth. My nipples are hardened from the sudden chill at my back. Pretty soon, he'll see the evidence.

With one hand, he grips my jaw. "Good. Don't ever lie to me again, *Kisa.*"

Never.

He pushes my skirt higher. His fingers yank my panties aside as he teases me with his digits. He leans closer, his breath tickling my ear. "Do you want me to fuck you?"

My lips part, but the words don't follow.

Mikhail pulls back, releasing me from his clutches.

"Why'd you stop?" My heart is pounding, slamming against my ribcage. I'd have given myself completely over to him to do with as he pleases.

He chuckles under his breath. "*Kisa*, you must answer me when I ask you a question." His thumb strokes my cheek, and I lean into his touch.

"I'll answer you," I say. It takes more energy than I ever imagined to speak, to voice the simple thought of 'yes' aloud.

His fingers guide me to the sofa, and he turns me around to face the arm of the couch. "Bend over," he instructs, guiding me forward as he lifts my skirt.

There's a coolness that caresses my skin as the air reaches my panty-clad bottom. He tugs the satin material down to the floor, and his fingers smooth over my ass before he paints my cheeks.

"Ouch!" I gasp and clench my buttocks. My eyes widen, and I pull away, standing up, covering myself. My skirt falls back around my waist. "Did you just spank me?"

He grabs me by the waist and puts me against him. His fingers slip under my skirt. "Spread your legs," he orders.

I do as he commands. "I ought to teach you a lesson for lying and betraying me," Mikhail says.

I inhale a sharp breath. "Are you going to spank me again?" The room feels a thousand degrees, and I have half a mind to discard all my clothes, but if he's going to put me over his knee, I'm not sure I'm ready for that yet.

"That is one type of punishment," he says.

Mikhail's fingers stroke me beneath my skirt, exploring my folds.

I exhale a sharp breath as his touch ignites a throbbing sensation at my core. It's rare that any man has brought me over the edge. Usually, they're fast, quick, and looking to satisfy only themselves.

But already, Mikhail is different.

"You're wet, *Kisa*. The punishment, while, usually, I find quite effective, I'm concerned that you might enjoy it a little too much." He smacks my pussy, and a low, guttural moan slips out.

The throbbing sensation only further intensifies, and Mikhail seems pleased with his accomplishment.

"Your punishment will be determined later," he grunts as he loosens his belt and unzips his slacks.

"Good," I whisper, letting my gaze wander lower.

Reaching out, I help him out of his pants and his boxers, and drop to my knees, wanting to take him into my mouth.

He grabs a fistful of my hair, bringing me back to stand. "Later," he says. "Right now, I want to feel your tight little pussy around my cock. I want to hear you scream my name."

My insides throb at his words, at his dominance. He's unlike any man I've ever slept with. None have ever been a member of the bratva, let alone the leader.

I undo two buttons on his shirt before he rips the material off, the white cotton falling to the floor. "You were taking too long," he says.

He's gorgeous, and while I'd seen him naked earlier, I hadn't been able to admire his chiseled abs and glowing physique. My palm caresses his chest and down his abdomen, feeling his muscles beneath my touch.

"Come with me." He leads me to the arm of the sofa. "Spread your legs," he whispers against my ear. Mikhail's hand guides me forward, pushing me down against the sofa, over the arm, as he thrusts into me.

He's not the least bit gentle or slow. And I'm grateful that we're both wanting the same thing. My fingers claw at the upholstered couch as I lean forward.

His cock pounds into me, and I reach around with one hand to touch my clit.

"What are you doing?" His voice is rough and sharp.

What the fuck does he think I'm doing?

"Throwing a party," I retort.

He laughs under his breath. Does he find that funny? It isn't supposed to be, but if he's going to get off, I want to too, damnit!

I don't stop my ministrations, letting my fingers circle my clit as he continues to pound into me, quickening the pace. I slam my eyes shut, and my insides quiver and tremble as the first spasms begin to quake, rippling through me.

Mikhail growls at me, shoving my hand away as he teases my clit with two fingers. "I'm the only one who will give you pleasure," he growls into my ear. "Don't ever forget that, *Kisa.*"

My hips gyrate with him, and with his other hand, he holds my waist as he thrusts harder, driving deeper inside of me.

I'm tinkering on the edge, and I want to break free. "Then, fucking let me come," I say. My breathing is raspy and thick.

Ordinarily, I'd hate being in this position, bent over the sofa, but with Mikhail, it's intimate, and he's in control. I've never relinquished power to anyone.

But I'd willingly submit to him.

I don't understand, but it turns me on.

He turns me on.

He bites down on my neck. The sensation drives me over the edge.

I clench down onto his cock. The spasms ripple through me, causing my insides to tremble and my heart to pound violently in my chest.

He grunts into my ear as he lets go, releasing himself inside of me.

I gasp for air as I stand and slowly turn around, wrapping my arms around his waist. "This can't be a thing between us," I say. I don't know what he's expecting, but if I want my job back, I can't be sleeping with Mikhail.

But it's more complicated than just my job.

"I'm pregnant," I whisper.

"Already? I don't think it works like that." He chuckles and kisses my forehead.

I shake my head. "I'm at least nine weeks pregnant, Mikhail. That's why I'm suspended from work, because I lied to my supervisors about what transpired between us. I disclosed to them that I am having your baby."

A flash of anger lights up his features. "You told them before you told me?"

I didn't know how Mikhail would react to the news, and having his involvement would change everything. I could no longer be an FBI agent. I would be forced out of my job.

"I wasn't feeling one hundred percent, and they sent me to see a physician. I didn't intend to tell them first, but I said something to Savannah, my coworker, and she dragged me into my boss' office. Then, the next thing I know, I'm suspended because of my conduct."

"I want you to move in with me," Mikhail says.

His answer catches me off guard. I just told him that we couldn't continue our escapades. I'm pregnant, and he wants me to pack up all of my shit and move in?

He can't be serious. "Are you crazy?" He must have lost his mind, and it's the endorphins making him give foolish suggestions.

"It's safer if you're here, under my roof."

We're not there yet. We're not even close to being at that point together. "That's not a reason to move in with someone. Besides, this was a one time thing. Right?"

His fingers dig into my hip, pulling me close against him. "I don't want it to be over. You're having my child. It is mine, right?" His voice is rough and deep.

"Of course, it's yours. I swear on my life. You're the father."

His other hand comes up to my cheek, and he pushes an errant strand of hair behind my ear. "I want you, *Kisa*. I didn't come by your house and bring you home with me to fuck you."

"Are you sure about that?" That is precisely what happened, whether he intended for it to or not.

He grabs my hair in his fist, lifting my jaw to face him. "Do you want to go home to your little date?" he asks with disdain.

"There is no date," I confess, my cheeks burning.

"If you don't move in with me..." he whispers and leans closer. His lips tease my neck, brushing against my bare skin. "...I can't climb into your bed whenever I desire. This game between us will be over forever. Do you know why that is?" he asks.

My breath catches in my throat. "Why?" I rasp.

"The Feds will be watching you. I can't take the chance that you'll go crawling back with information. Prove that you want me in your life and our child's life."

He crushes my mouth in a searing kiss before tugging on my bottom lip, pulling it between his teeth.

I whimper in response. All thoughts are momentarily fleeting as he stirs a warmth inside of me once again.

He relinquishes his grip on my mouth and lets me speak.

"Prove it how?" I ask.

"Choose me over them. Move in with me."

His gaze is dark, and he tilts his head, staring at me, awaiting my decision. "Choose you?" I whisper. Is it even a choice?

I barely know Mikhail, and the things I've read about him make him out to be a monster. The time that I've spent with him, I haven't seen that reckless and dangerous side.

I want to believe there are two sides to the man, a version that isn't quite so evil. Dangerous doesn't scare me. Maybe it should. He's not the sweet boy next door.

Mikhail is the man of nightmares that wake you up in a cold sweat.

I shouldn't want to be with him. I should run while I still can, while I'm still free. But I don't want to turn away from him. Instead, I submit to him. It's irresponsible and insane, but he saved my life, and the thought of him climbing into my bed whenever he desires stirs my insides in ways that it shouldn't.

"Prove your loyalty," Mikhail says.

"Haven't I already done that?" I ask. I slink out of his embrace and step toward my coat on the floor. I reach down, grab the wool jacket and slide my hand into the inside pocket, retrieving a flash drive.

"You didn't use it against me?" Mikhail asks, surprise evident in his voice.

"I swore my allegiance to you," I say, staring up into his darkened gaze.

He grabs my wrist with one hand, and with the other, I drop the flash drive into his palm. "No one knows your secrets. Not even me."

I never connected the thumb drive to a computer. It would have been easy to betray him, turn him in, and have him arrested. No doubt there is incriminating evidence, something linking him to all the crimes his men and he have committed.

"You protected me," Mikhail says, closing his hand around the drive. "You could have turned it over to the FBI, why didn't you?"

I honestly don't know. "I guess I'm not a very good agent after all," I say.

His gaze tightens. "I don't believe that for a second. Tell me the truth, *Kisa*."

I press my lips together. The truth is harder to say aloud. "I think when it was time to hand the flash drive over, I already started having feelings for you."

His features soften as a wry grin quirks at the corners of his lips. "Is that so?"

I shiver and grab my clothes from the floor. Without his body nestled up against mine, the room is colder.

Mikhail grabs his shirt from the floor. The buttons are strewn about, and he pulls the white cotton around my shoulders, letting it drape over me. "I like it when you wear my shirt."

"Why is that?" I ask, slipping my arms into the sleeves. I pull the front lapels closed.

"It's sexy having everyone know that you and the baby growing inside of you belong to me."

EPILOGUE

Madisyn

I resign from the FBI and take a full-time position at Steele Concierge Medical. Mikhail insists that I don't have to work outside of the compound, that he'd gladly pay me a salary as their on-call nurse.

Especially since I'm living with him.

But I don't want to be in that position again, sleeping with my boss.

Of course, whenever Mikhail needs me to handle a wound that one of his men acquires, I'm their first stop, especially if I'm at home.

Even at Steele Concierge Medical, they always seem to find me on the unit and end up becoming my patient. And in most cases, I don't mind it. The guys, while rough with others, are kind to me.

Probably because Mikhail would kill them if they weren't.

"We should grab drinks after work," Hannah says. "I'm dying to go dancing and have a night off. Mark is letting me have a girls' night. So, you have to come out."

I haven't disclosed to Hannah that I'm pregnant or that I'm living with my bratva boyfriend. Pretty soon, I'll have to tell her because I'll be showing. Well, the part where I'm pregnant. I'm sworn to secrecy about Mikhail being part of the bratva.

"Is he watching the baby?" I ask.

I don't like Mark. I can't explain it other than he rubs me the wrong way, but the two of them are engaged, and I don't want to be the friend to tell her that I think the man she's marrying is wrong for her.

Why can't that be her parents or her sister? Anyone else but me.

I know I'm a shitty friend.

"The baby is almost three, and she has a name, Bay." Hannah chuckles. She changes from her scrubs since our shift is over and grabs her phone from the locker. "Have you seen the pictures of Bay? Oh my gosh, she's getting so big, you have to see how much she's grown, and yes, Mark is watching the baby."

I slip into my black clogs, and she hands me her phone, unlocked to view her photos. I click on her library of pictures and cruise through all photos because she has tons. I scroll through the most recent and work my way back through her newborn photos.

"You'd better not have any naked pictures on here," I say as I scroll quickly through the photos on her phone.

"It's nothing you haven't seen, and no, Mark is a bit of a prude."

"That's too bad." I stop scrolling and drop her phone.

"Madisyn! If you break my phone, you're paying to have it replaced." Hannah slugs me in the arm.

I bend down, picking up her cell phone. Thankfully, the screen doesn't break, and the smartphone is still in pristine condition. "Who is this guy?" I ask, showing her the selfie shot of her and Luka together. What I'm asking is how does she know him?

"Bay's father. My hot one-night stand," she says and rolls her eyes, snatching the phone from my grasp. "I should delete that picture, but I thought that Bay may want to see it one day."

"And he's not in Bay's life. Why?" I ask again.

"The dick gave me a fake number and didn't work at the bar like he led me to believe. It's not like I even know if Luka is his real name. It's for the best," she says, her voice trailing off like she's trying to convince herself that she's happier.

Except I know that she's not. She's engaged to a man she doesn't even want to marry. I exhale a sharp breath. As her friend, I owe her the truth. "I know him, Hannah. He works with Mikhail. His name is Luka Ivanov."

The color drains from her face.

———

Thank you for reading Brutal Boss. I hope you enjoyed Madisyn and Mikhail's story! Continue the adventure with Hannah and Luka in Wicked Boss.

There's a darkness surrounding him, and I should stay as far from Luka Ivanov as possible.

Three years ago, I gave birth to a baby girl after one drunken escapade with a mysterious Russian bartender, Luka.

At least I thought he was the bartender.

When I went back to tell him that I was pregnant, no one knew who he was.

I've moved on... what other choice did I have?

The wedding is quickly approaching, and I'm engaged to Mark, a man I don't love. Don't get me wrong. He's sweet and kind, but a little too syrupy for my taste. I prefer my men darker, devious, and with a bit of bite. Mark is as vanilla as they come.

But I've settled because it's what's best for my daughter, Bay. She needs stability, and I want to give her the absolute best life that I can.

When my coworker stumbles onto a photo of my hot mistake, Madisyn confesses that she knows the Russian who knocked me up. I beg her to introduce us, but she has to swear not to tell him my secret before I do.

Wicked Boss is a standalone romance with a happily ever after. It is the second book in the Bratva Brothers series.

GIVEAWAYS, FREE BOOKS, AND MORE GOODIES

I hope you enjoyed Brutal Boss and loved Mikhail and Madisyn's story.

Sign up for my Willow Fox newsletter

If you enjoyed Brutal Boss, please take a moment to leave a review. Reviews help other readers discover my books.

Not sure what to write? That's okay. It doesn't have to be long. You can share how you discovered my book; was it a recommendation by a friend or a book club? Let readers know who your favorite character is or what you'd like to see happen next.

Thank you for reading! I hope you'll consider joining my mailing list for free books, promotions, giveaways, and new release news.

ABOUT THE AUTHOR

Willow Fox has loved writing since she was in high school (many ages ago). Her small town romances are reflective of living in a small town in rural America.

Whether she's writing romance or sitting outside by the bonfire reading a good book, Willow loves the magic of the written word.

She dreams of being swept off her feet and hopes to do that to her readers!

Visit her website at:

https://authorwillowfox.com

ALSO BY WILLOW FOX

Dangerous Boss

Bossy Single Dad Series

Billionaire Grump

Mountain Grump

Bachelor Grump

Faking it with the Billionaire

Looking for kinkier books? Try these spicy stories written under the name Allison West.

Boxsets

Academy of Littles

Western Daddies Collection

Obey Daddy Collection

The Alpha Collection

Western Daddies

Her Billionaire Daddy

Her Cowboy Daddy

Her Outlaw Daddy

Her Forbidden Daddy

Standalone Romances

The Victorian Shift

Jailed Little Jade

Prefer a sweeter romance with action and adventure?
Check out these titles under the name Ruth Silver.

Aberrant Series

Love Forbidden

Secrets Forbidden

Magic Forbidden

Escape Forbidden

Refuge Forbidden

Boxsets

Gem Apocalypse

Nightblood

Royal Reaper

Royal Deception

Standalones

Stolen Art

www.ingramcontent.com/pod-product-compliance
Lightning Source LLC
Chambersburg PA
CBHW021034030726
47496CB00006B/1537